FREDDIE THE BALLY

A TALE FOR OUR TIMES

Based on a true story.

Michael Leahy is an architect who lives with is wife Bróna in Clifden, Corrofin, County Clare. He first met Freddie Fox in Ballynahinch Castle in Winter 1995 and like most people who meet Freddie was immediately fascinated by his story. He has long been a visitor to the magic land of Connemara and to the enchanted Castle of Ballynahinch.

Freddie the Ballynahinch Fox 1997.

By Michael Leahy.

ISBN 0 9529830 2 8

Publisher :	Hero Press Clifden, Corrofin, Co. Clare. Tel : 065 - 21155
Printed by :	Colour Books Ltd., Unit 105, Baldoyle Industrial Estate, Baldoyle, Dublin 13.

Illustrations by William Gilchrist .
Cover includes illustration of Ballynahinch Castle reproduced by kind permission of Mr. Duncan Palmar.
Photographs of Freddie Fox by kind permission of
Mr. John O' Connor, Ballynahinch Castle Hotel.

To my wife Bróna, for her patience during the production of this book.

My thanks to the following :
To John O' Connor, Manager, Ballynahinch Castle Hotel, without whose generous help this book would not have been published.
To Paddy Honan for his help and patience in typesetting.
To Des Lally who introduced me to Freddie and told me his tale.
To all the management and staff of Ballynahinch Castle.
To Freddie and to foxes everywhere.

FREDDIE, THE BALLYNAHINCH FOX

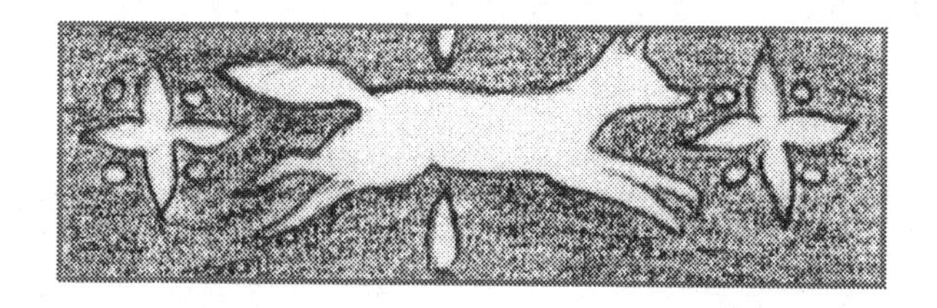

By
Michael Leahy.

Illustrated by William Gilchrist.

Based on a true story.

HERO PRESS

Foreword :

This tale is about a fox who became something of a celebrity around the area of Connemara some years ago, largely because of his association with Ballynahinch Castle, the former home of Dick Martin, the great 19th century campaigner for prevention of cruelty to animals.

I was lucky enough to meet Freddie on one occasion and insofar as it is possible for a human to get a story from a fox this is Freddie's story. The bits relating to humans I have changed around a bit, but the bits relating to foxes I have left more or less as they are.

M. L.

Clifden, Corrofin, July, 1997.

Contents

A pitched battle on the edge of the Vulpine Academy.
(see page 61)

CHAPTER 1;

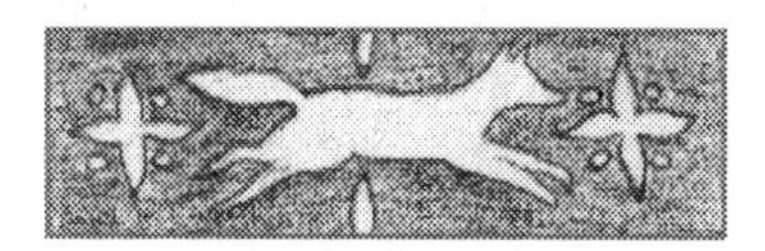

FREDDIE'S YOUTH AND EARLY LIFE.

This is the story of a fox by the name of Freddie. He became known as Freddie later on in his life, but in order not to complicate matters we will call him Freddie right from the beginning of the story.
Freddie was born to a large family of foxes in Connemara in the west of Ireland. Connemara is a magical,enchanted place, full of purple moors and wild rugged mountains, of beautiful lonely lakes and narrow sea inlets. The wildness and the beauty of the landscape is reflected in the inhabitants of Connemara, both human and animal, who are known for their daring and romance.

All the foxes in Connemara tended to have large families and Freddie loved to play with his brothers and sisters and his numerous cousins in the many out of the way spots and burrows that were to be found in his neighbourhood.

The first few months of Freddie's life after emerging from his den were spent in this sort of harmless play with other young fox cubs from the locality. It was a pretty carefree time really; off "gallivanting" as foxes call it, playing for most of the time, and then home to a feast of rabbit pie prepared by Freddie's mother Gert, a vixen renowned throughout the length and breadth of Connemara for the tastiness of her rabbit pie. Then curling up snugly in his nice warm burrow for a well earned sleep.
Many of Freddie's relatives from the East used to rib his

mother about her large litters.
"How do you think they will all last Gert? Rabbits and Ducks aren't as plentiful as they used to be, and what with all the new style fencing the farmers are using it's getting harder and harder to catch the odd chicken."
Gert used to listen apprehensively to this talk of food being scarce, but she always cheered up when she looked out through the window of her burrow and watched her cubs playing in the tall grass.
"The vixens in our family have always had large litters" she would reply "and all of our cubs have done allright so far." And so they had. Many of Freddie's relatives had been quite distinguished in the fox world and his family were generally known for their hunting skills and their fox-diplomacy.
When Freddie was nearly five months old, which is about nine years in human terms, the time came for the early, carefree days of his life to come to a close and for him to start preparing for what his elders called the rough and tumble of life as a fox in the wild.
He was brought by his parents to an institution known, rather grandly, as "The Vulpine Academy for Young Foxes".
While this sounded like a very stuffy sort of boarding school, in reality it was a clearing at the edge of Ballynahinch forest with lots of underground burrows which were used as classrooms. Freddie had to stay here for six weeks while some of the older foxes, the masters of the academy, taught him about hunting, how to raid farmyards, how to steal birds' eggs, and above all how to avoid being caught by human beings!
Freddie was lonely after his Mammy and Daddy at first . His mother had told him that the academy was going to be a place where he would have to work hard to learn all of his lessons. Both his parents had made lots of sacrifices saving rabbit skins and duck feathers to be able to afford the fees to send Freddie to this grand academy

and he was to work hard and graduate, possibly with a *magna cum yowla.* (Freddie later found out from one of the older foxes that this was a dog-Latin phrase meaning "with great howling" as all the other foxes at the academy were supposed to howl when a fox graduated with this special honour).

Shortly after his parents left however, Freddie found out that the discipline at the academy was quite lax, and the first thing that the young foxes did once their parents had left was to start racing around the warren of burrows that formed the classroom complex and playing hunting games.

Freddie was a bit surprised at this at first and was reluctant to take part in the fun as he felt that he must surely be doing something wrong. However when he saw that the teachers only made half hearted efforts to control the sport, Freddie soon joined in with the rest of the young foxes at playing such games as "Farmer Fool" (in which he got to play the farmer),"ducks and geese," "blind sheep dog" and "Polly parrot" a new game he had not seen before. Freddie couldn't help feeling a little guilty and felt sure that his parents would have been appalled to see such frolics after their many sacrifices. However Freddie was soon to learn that the first day's play-acting was something of an academy tradition, and that the real business of learning to be a grown up fox was to start the following day.

Some hours after their arrival all of the cubs, having run themselves into a state of near exhaustion, were brought by the kindly old porter, Dimplefleck, to their dormitories, girls to one side, boys to the other. "Dormitory " was too grand a word for it really as it consisted of a small room with a rammed earth floor in which all the cubs curled up together and slept soundly with an older fox on guard at the entrance. Even though it was a bit rough and ready, and very small, it was quite comfortable really, being lined with an assortment of goose and chicken feathers and having a little pool at one side where one could have a drink if thirsty.

That evening the cubs were all woken by a firm nip on the shoulder from Dimplefleck and were told that they all had five minutes to get ready, and then they would be taken to meet the masters of the academy. All the cubs yawned their sleep away, had a quick drink and started combing each others' coats with their fine teeth. Foxes, even at a young age, are very particular about their appearance and a very poor view would be taken of a fox who appeared in the evening without a properly combed coat and neatly polished paws. Some of the cubs were still involved in preening themselves when Dimplefleck returned and barked crossly at them to look lively as the masters were waiting. Those who weren't ready were nipped by Dimplefleck and chased out of the dormitory in no uncertain terms!
The cubs had to pass overground into the cool night air to get to the masters' assembly room. Now you may think it rather odd that the cubs were all getting up in the middle of the night to start their lessons, but when you remember that your fox is a nocturnal animal who only emerges to face the world in the middle of the night if he can help it, then I'm sure you won't consider their behaviour at all strange.

The cubs arrived at last into a large room with a small circular opening in the roof to let in the moonlight. This was a very splendid room lined with stone walls and was able to hold more than a hundred foxes together with the masters, who sat on a small raised stone platform. It looked even more splendid than it did on the brochures Freddie's parents had received when they were deciding where to send Freddie for his education. It was in fact the pride of the Vulpine Academy and certainly impressed all of the cubs, none of whom had ever seen any thing quite

like it before.
The history of the hall, as Dimplefleck never tired of telling them, apparently dated back to the middle ages, when it had been used as a lime kiln. It had then fallen into disuse and become overgrown until discovered by the founder of the academy, Slimlegs Greybrush, who had immediately recognised its suitability and set about its conversion.
In any event the foxes immediately lost their skittishness as they entered the hall and stood in awed silence waiting to be addressed by the stern masters on the stage.

The first address was given by the headmaster, an elderly and wise looking grey fox by the name of Slimlegs Whitepatch. It was another of the academy's many traditions that the headmaster adopted the name of the school founder "Slimlegs" along with his own. Whitepatch had been in charge of the academy for over three years now and was renowned for his wisdom and learning, especially in the area of getting the better of human beings.
His address was as follows;

"Young Cubs, You have been entrusted to my care over the next six weeks so that you can learn the skills you will need as a grown up fox in the wild and dangerous world. Among the skills you will learn will be hunting on land, hunting on water, rules and techniques for escaping from tight corners, the art of confidence, or how a fox can fool other animals without their realising it, and the very special techniques that are needed to get the better of human beings, the most resourceful and ruthless enemies that you will have to face. All of these things you will need in order to be able to survive and in order to be able to enjoy your lives as grown up foxes. Hopefully you will be able to pass some of these skills on to your own families when the time comes.

Your parents have made many sacrifices to be able to send you to our fine academy, and neither I nor the other masters here will tolerate any cub who does not apply himself diligently to his work and give his best efforts to his lessons. Even so I want to make one thing clear. We at the academy have a policy which has worked very well over the many years we have been in operation; We will not force a cub to learn, and any cub who is not interested in learning is free to walk out that window there at any time and go straight home to his Mammy and Daddy if he wants. Equally any cub who insists on disrupting the work of the other cubs will be sent home. If any cub does decide to leave I can guarantee you that he will live, though probably not very long, to regret that particular decision." said Slimlegs Whitepatch with a dry and somewhat sarcastic smile on his face. He continued;

"Now I have spoken about the skills you will need to be able to survive in life and to be able to make a living and to be able to escape from tight corners. However, I believe that the most important skills which you will learn while at this academy will be taught in the philosophy classes and that is why I will be taking these classes myself. In the philosophy class you will learn the rules of the foxes' code of honour and of upright behaviour. Many schools in recent years have tended to neglect this branch of learning, and I believe that this is something they will come to regret very much.
It is of course true that the fox code of honour can be hard at times and there will be many occasions during your lives when you will be tempted to break it. However a clear understanding of the code will help you as you go through life, and what is far more important it will help all of Foxdom which depends on good behaviour among all of its members in order to survive and to prosper."
After this the other masters on the stage set up a peculiar rhythmic screech of approval which lasted about

thirty seconds. The cubs attempted to join in but found that they were not able to give quite the same high pitched screech as the older foxes and participated in the "applause" by standing up and wagging their tails briskly, an action which is also recognised as a sign of approval in fox behaviour. They later discovered that the high pitched screech was something of an academy speciality which they would learn during the hunting class.

Most of the cubs had never heard anything quite like the head master's speech before. Foxes as a rule do not speak a great deal and tend to communicate by facial expressions, by leaving scent,(something that we humans know very little about) and by night calls. Apart from their story-telling season during September their conversation tends to be brief and limited to practical matters, as befits animals who spend large parts of their lives alone.

After the first part of the speech was over the headmaster introduced the various masters who would be taking the different classes.

The land hunting class was to be taken by a young fox from the Burren area in North Clare. His name was Fingal and he was a sleek, fit, no-nonsense looking fox with a striking red coat turning light brown at the tip of his tail. Despite his evidently young years he had the air of shrewdness which is common to most foxes who have to earn their living from the wild.

The water hunting mistress was called Fiona Firefly (or Fifi as she later intimated). She was really quite a stunner and many of the cubs instantly fell in love, as they thought, with her. She was a brown coated vixen in early middle age but had kept her good looks by strenuous exercise and sensible diet. She had a somewhat raffish appearance and could occasionally be seen wearing a monocle and smoking French cigarettes

Fiona was a vixen who liked to scandalise the other masters of the academy by her outrageous behaviour.

(even though this was strictly against the rules) with a long extendible cigarette holder!

The class called "Fooling Human Beings" was to be taken by master Reynard from France. Reynard was a rather lazy looking fox with a Brown coat who looked at you with a half closed eye and a slightly surprised air. Any one who thought however that Reynard was a fox who could be taken for granted or that his class would not be demanding was in for a pretty sharp surprise. Reynard spoke with a slight lisp that made his accent very attractive and his class, though hard work, was one of the favourites among the pupils.
The class called "escapology", or how to escape from tight situations was taught by an older fox called Mairteen from West Galway. He was very familiar with many of the traps and dangers in the locality and his class was based totally on practical work. Mairteen had had a somewhat tragic past which he never discussed but which could be seen in the firm set of his snout . Even though he didn't show his emotions too much he had a fatherly and protective attitude to the cubs in his charge.
The class known as "confidence" was taught jointly by a fox called Kelp Browntail and a vixen called Zowie Fisher. Confidence classes consisted of teaching a fox how to win the confidence of other animals, both bigger and smaller, and also how to swagger, how to pose and generally how to behave in a manner which was expected

of a young successful fox.
The philosophy classes were taken by the learned and somewhat fearsome Slimlegs Whitepatch, who, as you may have guessed, had no trouble in keeping order among his charges.
After the introductions the names of all the cubs were called out and they were divided up into groups. with about eight cubs in each group . One week was spent at each class, which is very different from the way you and I would have classes, but then foxes, like dogs, are very fond of getting stuck into things and like to master one thing before moving on to another.

One of the things Freddie found not too much to his liking in the academy was that the cubs had very little time for playing with each other, and the only free time they had was during a Sunday afternoon. Foxes, or fox cubs at any rate, love to play and frolic, especially just after the sun comes up, and you may often see them at their play in the early morning. Playing with other cubs is one of the earliest ways young fox cubs learn to hunt and fight, skills they learn to develop at places like the academy. Freddie found however that there was little time to play at his new school, and if ever one of the cubs was brave enough to complain to one of the masters he would be told stiffly that there would be plenty of time for playing when they had finished their education, but that as long as they were in the care of Slimlegs Whitepatch and the other masters they were to apply themselves to their lessons.

Despite the busy regime Freddie did have time to make a number of new friends . One of these was a very funny and slightly skittish cub by the name of Redeye. As it turned out Redeye was a distant cousin of Freddie and he felt that perhaps that was why the two hit it off very well as soon as they met. Redeye was a great mimic and was particularly good at imitating Mairteen the escapology master, with his slow gait and west of Ireland accent. Redeye loved to amuse the other cubs with his imitation of Mairteen in the dormitory during the middle of the day when Dimplefleck had fallen asleep.

The first class that Freddie was involved in was land hunting. Like most of the rest of the cubs he felt pretty sure that this would be an absolute cinch. After all, young foxes are all born (or so they think) with the ability to creep up quietly on their prey and to pounce almost like a cat. They also had lots of practice at a kind of "hunting" from their play with other cubs and with their parents. It was not surprising then that all the cubs approached the land hunting class as if it was well, slightly *infra dig.*
Fingal, the land hunting master, could sense a certain amount of disdain among his cubs as he led them out and he smiled wryly to himself. He had seen this kind of cockiness among first time cubs before and he had seen it disappear pretty quickly.
"All right lads and lassies" he began, "We'll start you with something simple. Lets say catching a mouse, that shouldn't tax your abilities too much. First, let's locate our mouse. Right, Redeye, off you go."
The cubs smiled at each other indulgently at the simple mindedness of their teacher. Every one knew that catching a mouse was pretty much child's play, or in this case cub's play. A fox's hearing is far far better than a human's and is so good that he can hear a mouse squeak at 100 yards. All the cubs stood stock still without making a sound as they had seen their parents do and Redeye pricked up his ears and began to sniff the air and move his head from side to side to see if he could hear or smell anything.
Suddenly he fixed his head in one position and padded stealthily to a small bush about fifty yards away with the other cubs in tow.

When he got to the bush he sniffed around carefully and finally spotted his mouse grubbing around at the bottom. It was then that he made his big mistake; he dived straight at the mouse making a great clatter in the process. Of course the mouse disappeared in double jig time.
This performance was greeted by howls of laughter from the other cubs. (A fox howling and a fox howling with laughter are two rather different things. The laughter is so high pitched that humans can hardly hear it. If ever you see a fox in a position with his snout pointing upwards and moving his head with a type of circular motion, but without apparently making any noise, then you will know that he is laughing at you, a thing foxes often have reason to do where humans are concerned!). When the other cubs were finished and the hapless Redeye, brush between his legs, was allowed to rejoin the group Fingal decided that he would give someone else a chance.
"Right, now that you're all so clever we'll let you show us how good you are. Let' see now, Freddie, you see if you can find the mouse that our gallant and resourceful friend", (here Redeye blushed almost as red as his brush, and was glad his coat was so fluffy so that no- one could notice).......“that our gallant and resourceful friend has managed to let slip through his paws"
Freddie felt that this would be no problem and he was really surprised that a clever cub like Redeye had let easy prey like a mouse make such a fool of him. As before, all the cubs remained stock still and Freddie pricked up his ears to listen for the sound of the mouse rustling in the tall grass or squeaking. It wasn't long before he picked up a sound, and then, after he had moved his head to a few different positions to get a "fix" as he had heard some of the older foxes call it, he headed straight for the point where the mouse was located with the others following behind. Just like Redeye had done before him, Freddie

dived straight for the mouse only to see his paws get tangled in the grass and to watch the mouse dart away. The laughter wasn't quite as hearty this time, and after Fingal had selected three more "volunteers" all of whom failed miserably to lay tooth or paw on their quarry, the cubs were beginning to look disheartened.

"Allright then my fine young hunters," said Fingal "the first thing to remember about hunting a mouse in terrain like this, is that your mouse , being small, has one or two advantages when it comes to long grass. Firstly, he can dive into little tufts that your paws may get caught in. Secondly, while your mouse is not a particularly clever individual, he can be fairly quick on his feet, so I think you may find a pouncing action, rather than a diving action may be useful. Watch this."
Fingal located his mouse in the usual way and padded off towards him. However when he got to about three feet from where the mouse was foraging he stopped short. After sniffing the air a little he crept around the back of the mouse and raised his head above the top of the grass and peered down on top of his prey. Then, instead of diving forward he leaped slightly upward and pounced straight down on top of the unfortunate rodent.
"You may have noticed" he said between chews, in that sarcastic way of his "that the fox is equipped with fairly powerful hind legs. Use them. God didn't give you a free gift for nothing. Now, Roundears Merriweather, you're next."
Roundears went through the motions as before and when she found her mouse she tried to do just as Fingal had taught her.
She came very close to catching her first mouse but just as she was about to pounce the mouse darted to one side and was lost in the grass.
"Not bad, Roundears, a nice pouncing style, but I'm afraid you made a bit too much noise. Don't worry you'll soon get

the hang of it." said Fingal.
After this Fingal sent the cubs off separately to go mouse hunting and told them to report back in 90 minutes sharp. (Foxes have a very good sense of time and are always very punctual. A very poor view would be taken of a fox who showed up even a few minutes late for a date or a meeting).
As they were going Fingal went over to some bushes and pulled out an old magazine which he had previously hidden there and began to "read" it until the cubs returned. Now you may think it rather odd that a fox would attempt to read a human magazine, but the fact is that foxes love patterns and shapes, and they adore looking at detailed pictures. Fingal spent his free hour and a half looking at the many pictures in the magazine. I sometimes think that foxes and other animals see a lot more in pictures than even we humans do.

The cubs returned at the appointed time, all of them arriving within two minutes of each other, and I'm afraid, with only limited degrees of success. Of the eight cubs who had gone out, only four had managed to catch any thing, and some of the catches were rather poor specimens and wouldn't have made more than a mid morning snack at the best of times.

"Not exactly the feast of the loaves and fishes" drawled Fingal as he rolled over on his back on some decayed grass. (The cubs were to find out the reason for this later.) "Before I go any further I think I should point out that at the academy we have a policy of self sufficiency. If cubs don't catch, they don't eat! Furthermore, as you are one of the hunting classes, you have the responsibility of catching enough food for the entire student body of the academy, and just to concentrate your minds we have a policy that the hunters don't eat till the others are finished."

The cubs looked haplessly at their meagre haul and began to feel decidedly worried about how they would be greeted when they returned that morning. They all looked rather sheepishly back to Fingal and began to regret their earlier bravado.

"All right, form a straight line there and I'll teach you few tricks"

Fingal lined all the cubs up and began by showing them the best types of pounces, crouches and jumps. He also taught them the best way to creep noiselessly and of course the importance of staying down-wind of their quarry so as not to give the game away by being careless about their scent. He described in detail the best scents to sniff out for, (foxes have a most extraordinary sense of smell), and gave them some advice about emitting scent if they got into trouble.

He then put them through a series of exercises to improve their pouncing and jumping. When this was over he gave them a ten minute break. (The exercises were quite strenuous and some of the cubs, including Freddie, were pretty tired.)

After this he sent them off again for another ninety minutes but this time he told them to stay within a half mile radius and that he would be prowling around keeping an eye on things. If any of them needed help or got into trouble they were to send a message by emitting some scent through their tail glands and he would come and help them. It was getting towards midnight and Fingal knew that there might be some other predators, such as barn owls, who just might be big enough to have a go at some of the smaller cubs in his charge.

Before they left he got them all to sit around in a circle, to join paws, and to growl together for about thirty seconds. This he told them was an ancient fox spell, but I think the effect was more psychological, to try to get them all into a good aggressive hunting mood.

The cubs then scampered off and commenced their

hunting, with special instructions to concentrate on mice. Again they were told to return in exactly one and a half hours.

All of the cubs were aware of the necessity of catching something and despite their tiredness they set out with great enthusiasm.

Freddie went deep into the forest making a careful note as he went of landmarks and particular scents so that he wouldn't loose his way. He went slowly, keeping his ears pricked up to catch any mouse sounds. It wasn't long before he came across his first quarry, a young mouse rooting in some weeds, presumably looking for berries or worms. Freddie crept up as he had been taught and pounced at exactly the right moment, leaving the poor mouse no chance at all. Freddie was delighted with himself, and was just about to start having a little feast when he remembered that his task was to find food for the others at the academy as well. He picked up the mouse and set off in search of more.

Over the next hour and a half Freddie came across a further six mice and one stoat. He managed to catch three of the mice making a total of four, but unfortunately the stoat skipped quickly to one side and raced off just as Freddie was about to pounce, and his chance of glory was gone. Freddie then set off with his four tasty little mice and headed back to the clearing where he knew Fingal would be waiting. Just as he was getting near the clearing he was distracted by a low purring sound, and going to investigate he came across a badger set at the base of an old Oak tree. There were three little badger pups and Freddie was just about to pounce when he heard a sharp call behind him.

"Freddie! Just what do you think you are doing?"

It was Fingal, who seemed to have appeared out of nowhere and was looking as stern and cross as Freddie had seen him all day.

" I.....,I just thought that these young badgers would

make a nice pie for Cook if...."
"I know exactly what you thought, Freddie Fox," said Fingal crossly "and I'll have you know that the Vulpine Academy is a respectable school which does not tolerate the unnecessary killing of young pups, only a few days old. If you want to learn that sort of behaviour then perhaps you should have gone to a business school instead of an academy! Now, come along at once and bring your mice with you."
Freddie was pretty taken aback I can tell you. His parents had never spoken to him like that. He put his brush between his legs and meekly followed Fingal to the clearing. He had heard abut the academy's somewhat "old fashioned" attitudes but he was at a loss to explain what he had done wrong. He thought it was terribly snobbish of Fingal, particularly as he himself was quite a young fox, to speak so disparagingly of business school. After all, business schools were all the rage nowadays and his parents had considered sending him to one. Still he thought, as he emerged into the clearing, better not to argue, perhaps he would understand in time.
Freddie was to come across many examples of this high handed teaching style of the academy over the coming weeks, and at times it was to cause him great annoyance, even anger, but he forgot about it now as he emerged into the clearing with his four fine, good looking mice.
Freddie and Fingal were the last to return, and Freddie was delighted to see that while all the cubs had caught something only two others from the class of eight had caught four mice, Redeye and a rather superior looking vixen cub called Banshee (what a pretentious name Freddie thought jealously). To be honest, Freddie thought that his specimens were the best of all.

They had another two sessions of hunting that night with each session followed by some tips from Fingal and then a brief rest period. About an hour before the sun was due

to come up it was time to set off back for the academy.
They returned home, all of them quite tired at this stage and with their guard a little bit down but Fingal kept a good eye out for danger, and stopped a few times as they were returning while he listened out for humans, dogs and other such enemies.
When they finally got back, they piled up their mice in a large pile in the middle of the great hall and as the other foxes finished their classes they would come and admire the day's catch. The water hunting foxes' catch was put in a separate pile alongside, and the two piles together certainly made a very impressive sight.
The cubs were then allowed some time off as Cook and her team prepared a buffet which would be eaten by the entire school.
While the other cubs, who had been at classes and practical demonstrations for most of the day, were quite energetic and started to play all sorts of games, the two hunting groups were quite tired and, for the most part lay down in front of the fire in the cubs' common room and chatted idly among themselves or just napped.
When the food was ready all of the cubs and masters assembled in the dining room and the procedure was that first the teachers, followed by the various classes, would go to the table and take their food away with them to their place in the dining room. The academy's cook, a kindly middle aged vixen by the name of Briarpatch, had a great fondness for old fashioned cooking and the academy's fare consisted mostly of pies, some fruit, and fish terrines. Freddie was certainly looking forward to his turn.
As Fingal had told them, the land hunting cubs had to wait till last , with even the water hunting team being allowed to go to table before them.
Before anyone started Slimlegs Whitepatch said a short thanksgiving prayer and gave a little homily about making good beginnings. The masters certainly made a

good beginning, thought Freddie as they were the first to go to the table and brought their food away with them to a corner of the dining room where they all sat together and discussed whatever it is that masters discuss.
After the masters the various other classes in turn went to the table and brought their food away with them and dispersed into little groups, some eating on the floor, some in little hollows and corners around the large dining room.
By the time the turn came for the land hunting class Freddie was dismayed to find that practically all of the good food was gone and all that was left for his group was about a quarter of one mouse pie, two bowls of Haw berries which were left over from last winter, one apple and a small trout, all of this to be divided between eight by now very hungry cubs! Freddie could see Fingal looking at them out of the corner of his eye with a "grim reaper" type of smile on his face and an "I told you so " look in his eye. Freddie couldn't help feeling that Fingal was getting a certain satisfaction out of the plight of the cubs. Still they all knew there was no point in complaining and they took what was left on the table and, dividing it out as best they could, they retired to a quiet corner and ate their humble repast in the silence of the afflicted. They all felt it pretty unfair that they , who had probably worked hardest during the day should receive such a scant reward and they didn't look forward to going to bed cold, hungry and unhappy.

After dinner was over the cubs had about thirty minutes free time and just as Freddie's group was leaving the dining hall Briarpatch emerged nonchalantly from the kitchen, and after first making sure that neither Fingal nor any of the other masters was watching she winked slyly at Freddie's group and made a barely perceptible flick of her left ear in the direction of the kitchen before disappearing into a nearby broom cupboard.

Fox cubs are pretty quick on the uptake and knew at once what was going on. They sauntered casually out in the direction of the meeting hall after bowing politely to the masters' group. No sooner were they out of the dining hall however than they doubled back down a corridor in the direction of the kitchen with Redeye leading the charge and Freddie in hot pursuit.

When they got to the kitchen Briarpatch and two of her sub cooks were waiting for them.

"This happens nearly every first day" she sighed. "I always think it so unfair the way the hunting cubs get so little to eat on their first few days. Fingal and old Slimlegs think it is all a part of the academy's discipline, but I think they just enjoy seeing you young ones suffer. Anyway I've a few bits left over here that you might like, but whatever you do don't breathe a work of this to another living fox or poor old Briarpatch here will be looking for another job, and probably without any references either."

She had a magnificent spread ready for them with a rabbit pie, two large and plump rats, some duck pâté if you please, and a pudding made of apples and ripe cherries, wherever she had gotten them. Whether they were breaking the rules or not the cubs didn't need a second invitation and they tucked in with gusto while Briarpatch and her accomplices kept watch anxiously at either door of the kitchen.

When they were finished they would have loved a good long stretch in the floor, but they were shooed out by Briarpatch who warned them "Remember, Mum's the word!"

Thus mollified, the cubs emerged into the common room and lolled around looking content and with sly knowing grins on their faces.

They were rattled a bit however when just as they were giggling contentedly among themselves Fingal crept up behind them and enquired sharply "Well, what are you lot

looking so happy about? Haven't had too much to eat have you?"
Most of the cubs were stumped for a reply and started looking guiltily at the floor hoping they wouldn't give Briarpatch away when Redeye piped up "Well actually Master Fingal, we were just plotting how we were going to catch at least twice as much tomorrow as we did today and have lots of food left over to fill our bellies. After all, with such an excellent teacher as you we can't fail to make an improvement, so even though we're hungry now we were just thinking how lucky we are really!"
After this bit of audacious cheek from Redeye it was all the rest of the cubs could do to keep a straight face under Fingal's stern stare.
"Good, good." said Fingal still sounding suspicious, "That's the kind of attitude I like to hear." and he went his way casting an odd glance over his shoulder.
When he was gone and out of sight the cubs fell about the floor laughing. "You're a cheeky devil redeye." said Freddie, "If one of us had cracked there we'd have been turfed out of the academy for sure."

A few minutes later Dimplefleck came around ringing a little silver bell and the cubs all retired to their dormitories.
Freddie's group all huddled up together the way foxes do when they are at home. Freddie was delighted that his first full day at the academy had passed off without any major trouble. He was pleased with the new friends he had made, and though many of the things that had happened to him he had found puzzling, he was looking forward to the remainder of his time at the Vulpine Academy. Like the rest of the cubs he was tired and in no time at all he was fast asleep and dreaming of adventures.

CHAPTER 2

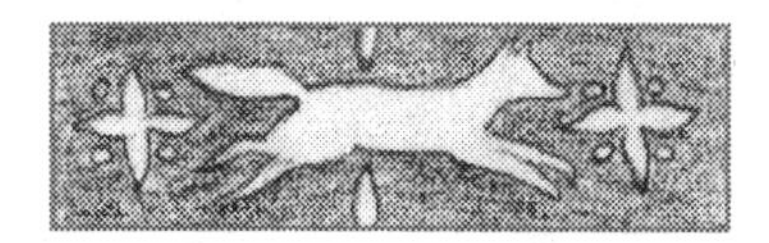

LESSONS AT THE FOX ACADEMY

After the uncertainties of their first day at school the cubs faced the following days with a much greater sense of confidence. It was just as well really, for as the masters never tired of telling them, it was very tough in the world out there and they were going to have to learn, and learn fast, if they were going to be able to fend for themselves come the following winter.

Freddie and Redeye, who were quickly establishing themselves as the gay young blades of the academy, (there were gay young blades every year sighed Slimlegs to himself as he watched them) didn't take all of this talk too seriously. After all they said, what was the point of being a splendid young fox with a magnificent tail if all you did was worry about the future. They occasionally spoke like this to the masters and were usually met with a disapproving shake of the head as much as to say "You'll learn one of these days my fine, bold little dog-fox!"

The land hunting classes got a good deal more complicated during the following days. The cubs were taught about edible fruit and nuts, which ones would last, which were poisonous and which ones were good for fox diseases like the mange or the scabies.

They were taught how to tell the signs of the weather. For example a lot of Haw berries in Autumn meant a bad winter coming and a prudent fox would make sure his dens were well lined against the weather, and if possible he would set up a little store for himself. Another trick was if they saw swallows flying low over the ground this usually meant that it was going to start raining shortly

and they might expect to find field mice trying to make their ways back home once the rain started.
They were taught how to watch a farmyard and the best times to organise farmyard raids.
They were taught the significance of various different types of scents at different times of the day and of the year. I'm afraid this is something I can't elaborate on too much as we humans know very little about the intricacies of the fox sense of smell. They have a much more developed sense of smell than we do and it is this that makes them "the masters of the night". They are quite comfortable wandering around at night sniffing about for danger and food, and are often amazed at how easily humans can be out-foxed on a dark night. To a fox his sense of smell is like our eyesight, and he will remember the smell of a place or of another animal much more quickly than he will remember what they look like.
One of the hardest things they learned was how to catch birds. Fingal would set them some tricky task like setting out a bit of bait for a sparrow and waiting in some tall grass to try to catch him. The rest of the class would wait at some distance to see how the "volunteer" was getting on and if he made a fool of himself the howls of laughter would start and he would have to rejoin his group with his head down and his brush tucked firmly between legs.

However it wasn't all learning by misadventure, and if a cub wasn't doing well Fingal would usually take him or her aside and work with them until they got their particular technique right.
Putting a few berries in a hollow tree trunk at nightfall and waiting for a foolish bird to go in was of course a favourite fox trick, but birds nowadays seemed to be very cautious, and if berries were plentiful a fox could find that his carefully laid trap would avail him nothing except perhaps a small shrew in the middle of the night. Then, if the bird landed and you didn't succeed in catching him,

that same bird would tell all his friends exactly where the fox was staked out and what his game plan was. Hunting birds was hard work!

Fingal, however,was something of a master hunter, and he had all kinds of elaborate tricks for catching plovers, wood pigeons and even ducks, a particular favourite of foxes.

" The most important thing a young cub can learn in the academy" Fingal would say when he had their attention "is the art of strategic hunting. I've known many's the capable fox starve to death during a cold winter when a bit of co- operation with his fellow fox and a bit of basic knowledge of the arts of strategy would have enabled him and his family to survive."

Fingal's strategic plans usually involved a number of foxes, often as many as five at a time, working together. Typically, the foxes would have to locate a group of say, ducks, who could be driven quickly into a covered area where they could be caught easily.

Two foxes who would be good at jumping would be stationed for example just under a group of willows close to where ducks were known to visit. When the ducks arrived and had their lookouts posted, these foxes, called "the sentries" would send for the other foxes known as "the runners" by emitting scent through their tail glands, a tricky technique that took some mastering. The runners usually would be chosen for their speed and for their ability to creep up on prey quietly.

Once the runners were summoned, they would approach as quietly as they could, and when they had observed the lie of the land, they would discuss among themselves the best way to attack and hatch a plan. Then they would creep up as close as they could to the ducks and as soon as they were spotted by the duck lookout, fox -runner number one would start barking his almighty best. The other runners would pop up at the same time to try to spread confusion among the ducks and drive them towards the low trees. The sentries of course would remain as quiet as humans in a church while all this was going on. It was very important to have steady foxes as sentries and not young skittish foxes who would start barking or screeching with excitement and in that way ruin everything.

If things went according to plan the ducks would be driven straight towards the low branches where they would have to fly low, and then up would pop the jumping sentries and snatch them out of the air. On a good hunt like that two sentries could snatch five or six ducks before they could regroup, and if the ducks weren't fast enough the runners might be able to catch them in what Fingal called a "pincer movement".

Fingal had many tales to tell of great hunters he had

Some cubs were inclined to be inattentive during classtime.

known in the past, such as Ginger Flash, the legendary "Flying Fox of Foynes" in west Limerick. Fingal claimed he had once seen this fox jump to a height of over eight feet to pluck a duck out of the air!

Group hunting was of course a good deal more complicated than I've explained it here and lots of quite tricky things like angle of the sun, time of year, wind speed and all sorts had to be taken into account. (Or so Fingal claimed any way, but I think he liked pretending that it was a bit more difficult than it actually was).

Fingal used to spend hours and hours teaching the cubs tactics for this "strategic hunting", and he used to draw complicated diagrams on a large stone "blackboard" at the side of a rock. Often, he got so carried away that he would completely forget about the class and when Redeye, who was a very good mimic, would make a noise like a weasel Fingal would turn suddenly and then realise that he had been more or less talking to himself for the last twenty minutes or so.

He would blink and smile at the class and say something like "Strategy is the greatest art any fox can know" and then come down to earth again and do some actual hunting, which the cubs enjoyed.

Most of the cubs were more inclined to hunt on their own rather than get involved in the complicated business of strategic hunting and a lot of Fingal's fine talk fell on deaf ears. Foxes have a strong independent streak and to this day it can be difficult to get them to hunt together.

Fingal's class was one of the hardest and most complicated classes, and while most of the cubs loved the first few days they were nevertheless glad to get something of a break and go on to the water hunting class taught by the ravishing Fiona, or Fifi, fox.

Water hunting isn't quite as important for foxes, mainly because they are much fonder of meat than they are of fishes.

Nevertheless Fifi taught them lots of tricks about what could be found to eat at the water's edge, especially down near the shallow inlets of Bertraghboy bay, or the disappearing lakes around Ballynahinch and Recess.
The main target of course was wader birds who are not as clever as ducks and a bit easier to catch. As well as wader birds, shallow lakes and lakes with changing water levels give a lot of opportunities for catching fishes who are stranded in shallow pools. The main trick is to watch for when a lake starts losing water and to try to identify where fish are likely to get trapped and move in before other predators like herons or gulls got in on the action first.
Fiona also taught the cubs a great deal about standing your ground in a fight and how to face an enemy down. "It's all about confidence" she used to say . "Even the biggest enemy may not be quite as brave as he may look or sound , and if you stand your ground and raise your brush as high as you can to make yourself look tall and fearsome you may easily come out on top."
The cubs found out exactly what she meant one morning as they were returning home with their catch when they stumbled across a large and bad tempered looking badger in a small clearing. The badger quickly manoeuvred himself into a position where he had Fifi and three of the cubs with their catch cornered against a large Beech tree. Badgers are notoriously strong and once a badger gets his fangs into a fox's hide that's pretty much it. The cubs were terrified and cowered up to Fifi. She however looked straight into the badger's eye and drawing herself up to her full height snarled full throatedly at her enemy. The badger who was bearing down on her was startled, and as soon as Fifi saw him hesitating she made a dive as if to go for his throat. The badger was so taken aback that he turned tail and ran, and didn't stop till he had reached the other side of the clearing.
"Come along cubs" sniffed Fifi as if nothing had

happened, "we'd better be getting back. There's a hunt ball on tonight and I haven't even got my make up on yet." The cubs, especially the young boy cubs, were lost in admiration at this coolness, and they all decided that Fifi was the neatest vixen they had ever seen.

Vixens could be exceptionally brave, especially when it came to defending cubs, either their own or others, and all of the boy cubs wished they would meet a vixen like Fifi when they grew up and got married.

The cubs spent four days with Fifi and then they graduated to the Escapology class with Mairteen. Mairteen didn't have quite the style and panache of their previous two masters but he was very solid and sensible and the cubs learned a lot from him and got to like him in the end.

Mairteen stressed the importance of knowing your locality intimately, and indeed he knew every square inch of the area around Ballynahinch. He always said that local knowledge was a fox's ace in the hole. If a fox was faced with a hunter with a gun or a pack of dogs his main chance was to lead them to somewhere that had lots of hidden traps or holes that the fox knew about, and to make his escape while his enemy floundered about.

"There's no point in being a dead hero" was one of his favourite sayings. "If your chances aren't good then the best thing to do is to beat a tactical retreat." Mairteen showed them ideal ground for leading dogs into, such as a marshy or wetland area with a few narrow passages through it. The best trick was to try to get onto your stepping stones through the marsh just before the dogs got there. If you then played dead as the dogs arrived they would be sure to get excited and rush straight for you without looking where they were going. Hopefully then they would end up knee deep in marsh while you could make your escape at your ease. Most foxes in this situation would stay for a while and have a good laugh at the dogs floundering about, but Mairteen wasn't too keen on this sort of bravado, and his advice was to get away as quickly as possible.

Another trick was knowing the height that other animals, particularly dogs, could jump. Hunting dogs could usually not jump very high whereas some foxes can jump nearly as high as a cat. If you were being chased by a pack of hunting dogs it was usually safe to jump onto a wall about five feet high. (Mairteen always used feet and inches, he had never gotten used to metres and centimetres and these other new fangled things like kilograms). However there wasn't much point jumping on top of a wall if it didn't give you a means of escape. If the dogs could surround you at the base of the wall you were in a right pickle.
Hunting dogs, though none too bright, are very determined, dogged in fact, and they could wait for ages, days sometimes, for a fox to come down off a wall. If a fox found himself in this situation his only hope was to try to attract another fox to come to his aid to distract the pack away while he made his getaway.
"However", Mairteen said sadly, "you may not always find it that easy to attract another fox to come to your aid. There may not always be one about, and the truth is that nowadays, foxes won't always come to the aid of another fox who is in trouble, even a fox they know."
The sad way in which he said this made the cubs wonder if he had experience of this kind of betrayal himself in the past, but Mairteen was a fox of few words, and he was not the kind of teacher who could be distracted by engaging him in conversation about past tragedies.
One of the most, if not the most important principles of fox escapology, is that of ensuring that you always had two routes of escape. Even the cubs knew before they came to the academy that you should never build a den without at least two entrances and preferably more.

Mairteen taught the cubs all about building dens; the right depth underground, how to ensure that your roof was strong enough so that it wouldn't collapse during the rains, the best way to space the burrows and passages, and how to hide the entrances from other animals and humans. Most foxes have more than one den so digging and building is very important. Lots of the cubs didn't like these lessons which weren't too glamorous and which were quite hard work, but as Mairteen used to say,
"Remember my fine dog foxes and vixens, you may be as good looking and as brave and as swanky as you like when you grow up, but if you don't know how to build a proper den then you'll never be able to protect your own family and you'll never attract a husband or wife."
Even cubs know how important a mate is , so they gritted their fine little white teeth and kept to their digging and shoring lessons.
Another of the subjects Mairteen taught was about knowing how to avoid human traps.
"If you ever have the misfortune to get caught in one of those devilish devices that human beings put out on land to try to catch us foxes, then you can be assured of a horrible, painful, slow and miserable death." he told a hushed audience of cubs one morning.
"The awful thing is that once caught there is no way out. You can scream and screech all you like, and even if you do attract other foxes to help you they won't be strong enough to open the jaws of the trap." said Mairteen, relishing the obvious fear he was causing among his pupils.
Mairteen then brought them out to where he knew some traps had been laid so that he could show them what to look out for.
"Now tread carefully boys and girls, we don't want any nasty accidents" he said as they approached the area in question. Mairteen led the way and padded around very carefully sniffing for human scent as he went. He was

looking for disturbed grass or other tell-tale signs such as broken twigs, and it wasn't long before he uncovered a trap about two feet wide with particularly sharp looking teeth.
"This is a classic example of what humans can get up......."
Mairteen noticed something out of the corner of his eye and turned sharply.
"Roundears Merriweather " he barked "Stop dead where you are!"
Roundears, who had been feeling a bit off that morning and hadn't been paying too much attention, stopped dead as she was told with her front right paw in the air.
It was just as well for her that she did because Mairteen uncovered another trap right where she had been about to tread. He pulled her roughly to one side and then made her wait beside the trap while he went off and got a large tree branch.
He then threw the branch onto the trap so that it sprang shut just inches in front of poor Roundears' nose. The other cubs all sprang back at the noise it made and Roundears went as white as a sheet! (Under her silky coat that is).
"Now for goodness sake Roundears what did you think you were doing, wandering around like a lost sheep in a place you knew there were traps laid. You'd better buck up a bit my fine silky little vixen if you want to graduate from this academy. One more performance like that and I'll have you sent home!"
Roundears Merriweather was almost in tears, but she certainly kept a very careful lookout for the rest of the morning.
When Mairteen had calmed down he showed them some other tell-tale signs to look out for in traps, such as cut grass placed as a camouflage, and small bits of meat bait. He also showed them how to spot snares and how to help another fox who was caught in a snare.
As they were going Freddie suggested that they should

set off the rest of the traps to save other foxes being caught.
"Well done Freddie" said Mairteen, "that shows you are thinking about your fellow fox. Very commendable. However, we don't want our human friends to become aware of the fact that we have "foxed" them , now do we? After all if humans realise that we can set off their traps, they'll just come up with something even more nasty and cruel, something we mightn't be able to figure out. However, we may be able to set a few "counter-traps" of our own."
The cubs then got to work in doing what Mairteen described as "covert anti-camouflage" which involved scuffing up bits of grass, breaking off loose branches from nearby trees and leaving obvious bits of scent about. This would leave signs for other foxes that there was danger ahead without letting the humans know that their traps had been rumbled. After this bit of good work they set off for home feeling well pleased with themselves.
As they were approaching the academy Mairteen suddenly stopped short again. He gingerly went over to a low bush and pulled its branches back. There was a sight that shocked all of the cubs to the core, an old grey fox with his front paw caught in a trap. Mairtin sniffed around a bit and then bowed his head and said a short fox prayer.
"Come on cubs, there's nothing we can do for him. He's been dead about two hours." said Mairteen softly. "Come along. Follow me. Quickly now, don't look back."
The cubs went back towards the academy with their heads down. They were learning fast that fox life wasn't all fun and gaiety.
Mairteen looked terribly sad for the rest of the day. Rumour had it that two of his own cubs had been killed in traps and Mairteen had kept them alive as long as he could before the farmer had arrived. This in fact was why he hated traps so much, and why he gave a lot of time to

them in his class.

Mairteen was one of those foxes who didn't have much time for the company of other foxes, and at dinner time while the other masters would chat together, Mairteen could often be seen sitting alone, looking wistfully into space.

That night in their free half hour after dinner Freddie, who was out taking a walk in the cool night air, came across Roundears Merriweather huddled up under a bush sniffling to herself. When Freddie asked her what was wrong she replied between sobs;

"I don't think I'll ever master all the hard things we have to learn at school Freddie. Look how close I came to disaster this morning with that trap."

"Don't you worry Roundears, you'll soon get the hang of it. Everyone feels that things get on top of them sometimes. You'll graduate allright, you'll see" and he started playing a game of scratch with her and nipping her ear. That cheered her up allright.

Freddie liked Roundears and thought she was quite bright, even if she could be a bit of a goose at times. And he was very taken by her nice roundy ears!

Lots of the cubs around that time began to feel that the work at the academy was too hard and that they would have difficulty learning all they had to learn. They began to realise also that being a grown up fox was not all rabbit pie and duck feathers, and could be a dangerous and difficult business.

Foxes however are an optimistic lot for the most part and don't let the troubles of the world get them down too much or for too long. Freddie had learned from his father the importance of being cheerful, and the importance of cheering up another fox who had fallen on hard times. "Always try to build a fellow up" his father used to say. "Never lose an opportunity to say something nice to another fox, because we all need cheering up sometimes, and the happiness you spread now will come back to you

later."
Freddie hadn't fully understood this but all of his family had always been cheerful and now at the academy he used almost without thinking take time to cheer up cubs who were falling behind with their lessons, and he always managed to have a kind word to say or a foolish skittish game to play. This made him very popular with the other cubs at the academy and cubs who wanted to be cheered up or who were lonely for home would seek out Freddie, or Redeye who was another cheerful cub, and soon a game or some other bit of "divilment" as Redeye used to call it would start and the cubs would be back to their frolicking carefree selves playing hide and seek among the burrows of the academy or thinking up tricks to play on the masters.

It was well known that one of the masters, Kelp Browntail, had a great fancy for Fiona the water hunting mistress, though even the cubs could see that she had no interest in the world in him. Redeye devised a plot to make Kelp think differently however. Foxes, when they want to attract the attention of a mate, would never just walk straight up to them and say so. That would be regarded as pretty much social death and would ruin your chances with that fox or vixen forever more! Foxes place great store by what they call "proper courtship decorum" and usually leave subtle signs lying about for the mate they wish to attract. For a fox the ability to understand these signs is considered very important, and usually if your potential mate picks the signs up wrongly then all kinds of rows and confusion can ensue. In the previous year's mating season, Kelp had done practically everything he could think of to attract Fiona's attention, even going so far as to leave some of his throat scent immediately outside of her apartment. It was all to no avail however and Kelp's love remained unrequited.
Redeye wasn't in the academy two days when he realised

what was going on and decided that this tale of one sided love presented a great opportunity for some "divilment". One day just after the cubs had all gone to bed and Dimplefleck had gone to sleep, Redeye woke Freddie, Roundears, Banshee and another cub called Prancer and said "Right lads, I have a mid-day raid planned." They crept out as quietly as (or more quietly than) mice and padded off straight to Fiona's apartment.

A daring raid, carried out for the purpose of oiling the wheels of fox romance.

Redeye knew that she had gone out that day as she had mentioned going to a fox theatre in Galway with a friend of hers (whether male or female was not disclosed) to see the latest hit play, "The murder of the owl in the Hollow Tree" by J. B. Foxley. Redeye put Banshee (who wasn't at all approving) "keeping ducks" which meant keeping a lookout, while he, Roundears and Freddie dug open the door to the apartment and started rooting around inside. It wasn't long before Redeye found what he was looking for, Fiona's monocle, one of her most prized possessions, which she had got on a raid on Glebe castle house, an old farmhouse in south Mayo. Leaving the apartment they carefully replaced the entrance door and then dragged some decaying leaves over their steps to cover up their scent.

Then they padded off to Kelp Browntail's apartment. You've probably guessed what they were up to. When they got there Freddie put his ear to the door and listened intently. Foxes of course don't snore, but they do emit a slightly high pitched sound if they are having dreams and it was just such a sound that Freddie heard now. Redeye was all for breaking into the apartment and putting the monocle under Kelp's pillow, but Freddie and Banshee counselled caution and it was agreed to put it into his letter box so that he would find it first thing in the night when he checked his dispatches from Slimlegs Whitepatch which were usually sent out in the middle of the day.

Having done their work they crept back to the dormitory and curled up together but could hardly sleep with the excitement and the thought of the fun they had had and what would befall the following night.

The next evening as the cubs were going out to class they decided to pass, nonchalantly of course, by Fiona's apartment to see what they could see, Redeye coolly humming a tune as they went. Fiona was sniffing about her entrance as they passed by, and eyed them suspiciously.

"Lucky you thought of that trick with the leaves, Prancer"

said Freddie. Shortly afterwards they bumped into Kelp Browntail. Now Kelp was a fox who was very fond of what foxes call "posing", that is putting on a bit of a show, and boy, oh boy, ***was he posing tonight!***
Now posing and swaggering were among the subjects Kelp used to teach, but on this occasion he was at it with particular aplomb; tail at a raking angle and curling just so, toenails beautifully polished, coat immaculately brushed and not a rib of fur out of place. Not only that, he was wearing a spotted green dickie bow and ***a silver coloured waistcoat.***
It was all the cubs could do to keep from sniggering right in front of him and his attire caused a great stir among the rest of the academy.
That night at dinner Kelp made sure he sat right down beside Fiona and it was clear to the cubs that he was starting his courtship play. She of course was polite, as teachers are obliged to be to one another, and she may even have been flattered by his attention but it was plain to everyone who took an interest, (everyone except Kelp that is) that while her demeanour was polite, it was certainly not romantic.
Fiona got up to leave and then Freddie and his group excused themselves from their table and got ready to watch the fun. Fiona was making her way to the teachers' common room and Kelp, after first making sure that they would be alone, followed her in. The cubs had taken up their position at a safe distance behind the roots of an old oak tree and as Kelp entered they could see him checking something in the fob pocket of his waistcoat; **It was Fiona's monocle!**
The first thing the cubs heard was Kelp's sweet and pleasant tones and then a long pause. Then Fiona's voice: "So it was you!" Then Kelp's voice only more firm this time. Then all hell seemed to break loose and there was literally skin and hair flying. The cubs couldn't see exactly what was going on but could hear enough to

realise that both sides were giving a pretty good account of themselves.

Shortly after this who should come up the corridor but Slimlegs Whitepatch himself, with a fearsome look in his eye. He was wielding his umbrella and looking as if he was going to sort out the cub who was causing all this commotion in no uncertain terms. His umbrella was not an implement he used to keep off the rain, because most foxes don't mind rain too much, but to give an unruly cub a crack across his snout if law and order looked like breaking down.

The cubs under the oak tree roots crouched down in terror and you can imagine their relief when they saw that old Slimlegs realised that all the racket was coming from the teachers' common room. In he marched with his umbrella between his paws ready to strike the first thing that got in his way. His booming voice could shortly be heard resounding throughout the whole academy and soon the entire school , teachers and all, had gathered to see what was gong on.

Eventually order was restored in the common room and then silence and later Slimeg's voice hissing at his two masters. After another short period of silence Kelp Browntail emerged, his bow tie in disarray and his beautiful waistcoat torn. He didn't utter a bark or a screech to a single fox but put his head in the air and marched away. Some seconds later Fiona emerged, not looking a whole lot better, her coat severely ruffled and her brush in complete disorder. She looked about her, put her now retrieved monocle in her eye, and marched off in the other direction.

Then Slimlegs came out, his face giving a fair imitation of one of the more unpleasant types of thunder storm! He glared crossly at the assembled school who didn't have to be told what to do but immediately scattered in various directions to avoid the headmaster's anger.

I needn't tell you that this incident was the talk of the academy for the rest of the term, and was even referred to for years afterwards among cubs as "the night of the teachers' brawl".

Freddie and his friends, who were the only ones who knew the full story, decided that they'd better keep quiet until the dust settled, and it was only years later that Freddie told the full story of Kelp Browntail, Fiona Firefly, the dickie bow, the silver waistcoat and the missing monocle.

The next class that Freddie had to take was that of "Fooling human beings" taught by the French master, Reynard.

This was one of the most popular of the classes and was mostly held in classroom 1 C. This was a large dusty burrow just beside the main hall, and in fact Reynard often used the main hall for enacting scenes to teach the cubs the various tricks they needed.

One of the first and most elementary tricks that cubs had to learn was that of what he called "looking cute".

"It is important to remember that in human eyes the fox is an extremely beautiful animal. While humans are of course a ruthless lot, and for the most part won't hesitate to behave in a cruel and hurtful manner, nevertheless they have a certain appreciation of beauty. They also have a sentimental attachment to some animals and if you are surprised by one in a difficult spot your best policy may be to look as quiet and inoffensive as possible. In this way the human may be taken aback for a while and it is this split second element of surprise that may give you the opportunity to escape"

Humans didn't sound too bad from this initial description but Reynard was adamant that a fox would be very foolish indeed if he was taken in by a human. "Make no mistake about it " he would often say, "the human is the most ruthless and terrible enemy that any fox can face. If you can avoid them at all make sure you do so, and if you do get close to them then get away as fast as you can. I could tell you stories about the activities of humans that would make your fine cub's hair stand on end. Why, *Sacre Bleu*, when I was in France .....but no, I had better not tell you innocent little ones tales that would disturb your sleep" he said darkly.

Reynard had come over from France during the great fox and farmer wars of the 1980's and he would occasionally tell tales of the guerrilla warfare he had fought during those difficult days. Redeye was particularly good at getting him to waste a bit of class time in this way.

Looking cute wasn't as easy as it sounded, and involved putting a doe eyed look on your face, (a thing most self respecting foxes most definitely did not like) and ruffling up your coat in such a way as to make you look what Reynard called "cuddly".

Another Reynard speciality was playing dead. This was mainly to be used if you were being attacked by humans with guns. If a bullet whizzed over your head you could drop down and pretend to be dead. Usually if this happened the humans would slow down and possibly not bother to reload. Then up you could pop and make good your escape while they were a little off guard. You had to get your timing exactly right though, as if you hadn't fooled your human you would certainly make a very easy target lying on the ground.

"It is very important to, how you say, play to your strengths" Reynard used often say to them. "Remember that you have a very much better sense of hearing than either the human or the dog, and certainly a much better sense of smell, so if you keep your ears cocked and your nose open you will be likely to spot your human before he spots you. The human smells a bit like a wet pheasant; It's smell you will get to know soon enough. Remember

Master Reynard would sometimes tell the cubs about his exploits during his fighting days in France.
However many of the cubs felt that these tales were highly exaggerated.

also that humans can get quite excited when they are chasing foxes and if you keep your head you'll find that he gets easier to fool as time goes on."

One day Reynard took the cubs up to a high ridge about two miles from Ballynahinch castle. He sniffed the air very carefully before arranging the cubs in a line along the top of the ridge. They were looking down into the long valley of Derryclare, and they could see a great distance, almost all the way up to Kylemore lake, beside the old abbey.

After a while they could see a fox down below in the valley looking anxiously over his shoulder as he ran along the valley floor at the edge of the lake. It wasn't long before they understood the reason for his concern. They heard a high pitched bugle and soon they could see a pack of snow white hunting hounds pursued by about thirty humans on horseback in brightly coloured clothes and what Freddie thought were the most ridiculous tall hats he had ever seen.

"The West Galway hunt" said Reynard grimly. "They're always out this day of the year."

The hunters had seen the fox and were in full pursuit. As the hounds passed by in the valley, about fifty yards below them, the cubs' coats stood on end. There were about fifty hounds in all and there was no doubt that if they caught the fox they would rip him limb from limb. The hounds were well fed , strong about the shoulders and jaws, fast looking and rapidly becoming frenzied.

"Don't worry, *mes braves*," said Reynard when he saw some of the cubs becoming a bit apprehensive, "there is a particular wind eddy up here that I discovered a few years ago which causes the wind to, *how you say*, reverse. Right now, even though you wouldn't think it, we're downwind of them and there's no danger that they can smell us."

A few moments later the horsemen rode by and the cubs

peeped out to get their first close up glimpse of their worst enemy. Freddie had to admit that, despite their silly hats they looked pretty dashing galloping along, jumping over rough ground, some of them falling off and getting onto their mounts again. As they got closer however he could see that they had a hard, cruel set about them. Two riders broke off from the main group and galloped up along the high ground no more than seven or eight yards below them. The cubs kept their heads down but Freddie and Redeye peeped out just as the hunters passed by. They were so close that Freddie could see the whites of their eyes. One was a young woman with a steely and cruel look in her eyes and the other was a portly middle aged man who was lashing his horse without thought. Freddie remembered their hard eyes and he felt that all the terrible warnings he had heard about humans were well worth taking seriously.

The hounds in the meantime were beginning to gain on the fox who was looking about desperately for a means of escape. The hounds, sensing that a kill was near, began to bay madly. The ground was open and hard and there were few places for the fox to try his tricks of leading the hounds astray. Suddenly he turned sharply to one side and disappeared into a small mound about two hundred yards from the edge of a grove of trees. In less than a minute the hounds and hunters were gathered about the mound and things were looking bad for the fox. One of the hunters took down a small cross looking dog, a Cairn terrier, from his horse. This dog then disappeared into the mound in pursuit of the quarry while the hunters waited above.
"Not much chance for him I suppose" said Freddie sadly.
"I'm not so sure" replied Reynard slowly, "I know that particular fox , he comes from north Clare, and they are particularly good at the underground tricks in that part of the country."

While the hunters were gathered around the mound waiting for the terrier to do his work the cubs could just make out the sight of the fox emerging from an opening in the bank of a small stream about fifty yards away. It was all the cubs could do not to cheer, but Reynard warned them to keep deathly quiet and not to give their colleague away. The fox, who had escaped through a swallow hole into the dried up stream, crept quietly along the stream bed making for the forest about two hundred yards away. He was about fifty yards from the trees when one of the hounds perked up his head and started barking furiously. The fox had been spotted and the chase was on again!

Off the hounds raced madly in pursuit of their prey and the riders began to remount hurriedly. Freddie and his friends watched the fox's race to the trees willing him on all the way. They knew that while dogs could easily outrun foxes over a long distance a fox is well capable of a surprising burst of speed on a short run. The pack however were picking up speed and were starting to gain. Freddie could hardly bear to look, but then he realised, yes, their man was going to make it! The fox was running at his level best and he made out the forest with a good five seconds to spare on the hounds. He was home and dried once he got into the trees and though the hounds followed for a while it was clear that this was one fox who had escaped the west Galway hunt!
The hunters regrouped and headed off in another direction, and the cubs went home pleased that on this occasion at least their colleague had won out.
"A good lesson *Mes braves*, never go to ground unless you have another way out." said Reynard on their way home.
That evening at dinner the hunt was all the talk of the academy and all the masters and cubs gathered round to hear Reynard give a gripping and exciting account of what they had seen. They roared their approval and

howled with laughter when Reynard described the hunters gathered round the opening with their terrier as their quarry made good his escape. Foxes love a good story and Reynard was a particularly good *raconteur,* adding in lots of colourful detail.

After finishing Reynard's class the next set of lessons, taught by Kelp Browntail and Zowie Fisher, was that of "Confidence". This involved teaching the cubs how to be confident in themselves, and also how to win the confidence of other animals such as chickens or cats. This was a class that most of the cubs found very helpful and many of the feelings of trepidation they had felt earlier began to disappear as they began to develop the swagger and confidence for which foxes are renowned.
Kelp and Zowie taught the cubs how to swagger, how to take other animals by surprise with an apparent display of nonchalance, and how to "pose". Posing was a technique which foxes used mainly to attract other foxes. It involved an elaborate series of walks, waves of the head and eyebrows, subtle movements of the tail, discreet screeches and of course the judicious use of scent from the fox's various scent glands.
Cubs were taught how to understand the various messages that would come from foxes of the opposite sex (for this part the classes were divided in two in order to avoid embarrassment), and how to attract foxes of the opposite sex. They were taught fox dancing, fox singing and fox "raconteuring", which is all about the way foxes tell stories to one another. They were taught other things too but foxes are often embarrassed to dwell upon such things and they don't tend to talk about them much.

Winning the confidence of other animals was a thing foxes used in order to get a dinner when the hunting wasn't going too well. The fox would pretend to play with say a cat, and would keep a distance from them so as not to arouse any suspicions, and then as the cat got more and more relaxed they would gradually sidle up to them and, well-curtains for the poor old tabby! Some cats of course would have the good sense not to get close to a fox unless there was a tree nearby which would afford them a means of escape, but not all cats are quite so clever.

Now you may think this business of tricking other animals a fairly nasty way of going about your business, but that isn't the way a fox would look at it at all. The fox spends a great deal of his life being hunted and often has to go hunting himself by whatever means he can in order to feed both himself and his young ones. He has to use his guile where the badger may have his strength and where the hawk may have his wings and his eyesight. Foxes will often try to give other animals a fair chance, but after all, they must eat.

The confidence class also taught the cubs to be optimistic, to try to keep their tails up even when things weren't looking good and always to try to cheer up another fox who might be in difficulties.

Another important thing for foxes was always to have the laugh when they got the better of another creature, particularly a human being. They were obliged, if they had succeeded in fooling a human being, to sneak back and have a good laugh at them. For example, the fox who had escaped the west Galway hunt had followed the hunters at a distance and when they were on their way home he had jumped out in front of the horse riders and laughed in his foxy way in full view for about five seconds from a high bank above them. This had caused great consternation among the hunters (the hounds had already passed) but the fox disappeared again before they could re-organise.

When Freddie had completed the confidence class he was coming towards the end of his term at the academy. He now felt like a mature and confident young fox rather than the callow cub he had been only a few weeks earlier. He had one more class to go through however: The philosophy class, taught by the formidable headmaster Slimlegs Whitepatch. Freddie had always had a certain trepidation before Slimlegs and he wasn't looking forward to starting his class. As things worked out however he was to find Slimlegs' class one of the most interesting and rewarding of all.

CHAPTER 3

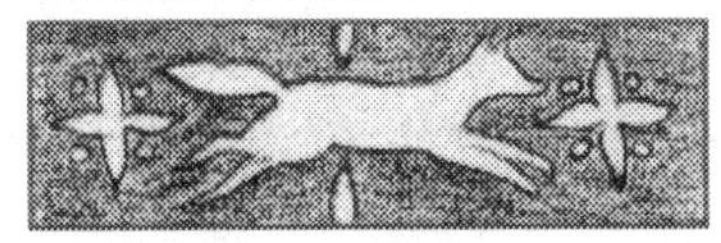

THE FOX PHILOSOPHY CLASS.

The philosophy classes, as the name might suggest, did not involve a great deal of practical work and were held indoors during the middle of the night and extending into the early part of the morning. Most foxes enjoy watching the sun come up , and Slimlegs Whitepatch, despite his forbidding manner, was no exception.

The classes were held in a large burrow with room for about 12 cubs and a raised dais for the master. The burrow had one hole in the ceiling for ventilation, as with the great deal of talk that went on cubs were wont to fall asleep if they didn't get their share of fresh air. A large rock served as a blackboard which Slimlegs used to illustrate the more difficult points.

Now what, you might well ask, is the use of philosophy to foxes? This was a question Freddie had heard his own father and some of his family friends ask when they got the brochure detailing the various subjects Freddie would be taught at the academy. Indeed you may often hear human beings ask the same question. (About the use of philosophy for humans, I mean, not the use of philosophy for foxes). Slimlegs however, in a very interesting series of lectures outlined the practical usefulness of fox philosophy for the survival of the fox species as a whole.

"It is important" he would often say, "to raise your minds above that which concerns you immediately, and to think of higher things such as the fox brotherhood and the concept of fair play to other animals and yes, even to humans on occasions."

This would not only help foxes to have a more meaningful life but would have many practical side effects as well. Or

so Slimlegs claimed at any rate.
Slimlegs was a very dignified older fox. His whiskers and the fur at the sides of his ears was beginning to go grey and this immediately instilled him with an air of authority among the cubs. Despite his years he was still a very handsome fox with a long, learned snout and thoughtful milky brown eyes, and many's the vixen cub who passed through the academy modelled their future mate on old Slimlegs. He had a pair of half glasses which he used to put on at the beginning of each class and he used to peer out at his charges in a way that made each cub think he was addressing his words directly at them. (In fact his glasses were something he used purely for effect; his eyesight was perfect but he felt that his glasses added to his air of authority. Even old foxes are very concerned about their appearance like that).
Even though Slimlegs had a severe manner, and stood no nonsense from any cub who wasn't doing his best, nevertheless he could have a kind word when it was necessary and most of the cubs got to like him even though they were always a little afraid of him.
Fox philosophy wasn't all about ideas. It involved a lot of rules of behaviour; how you should behave to another fox in a given situation, how to behave to other animals, what parts of the countryside should to be respected, and many other things too complicated and difficult to go into here. Slimlegs drilled his cubs very thoroughly and made them learn a large number of rules off by heart.
These were some of the rules they learned;

1. Never attack other foxes:

It's a peculiar thing but you may have noticed that foxes rarely fight among one another. They'll fight lots of other animals and can be great fighters when their backs are against the wall but they seem to accept that as a species they have enough natural enemies without fighting each other as well.

2. Never attack very young animals:

This was a rule that some of the cubs found hard to understand. After all, if they were hungry and needed to eat, what else were they to do? However Slimlegs was most adamant on this point. All animals should be given a fair chance in this life to have some time "to make their mark" as he put it, and for that reason you should never attack creatures who were still only pups or were totally helpless.

Slimlegs used to tell the cubs that it was important for cubs to be good just for the sake of it, but he would also issue them with dire warnings that if they continually broke what he called the Fox Code of Honour, that the forces of nature and of God would turn against them and that their lives would be made miserable.

Many of the cubs would be quite frightened at the tales Slimlegs had of the dire consequences that would befall them if they did not behave properly and the stories he had of the miseries that had been visited on foxes who had led dishonourable lives.

Slimlegs seemed to get great enjoyment out of telling the cubs frightening tales and he would tell with particular relish stories of foxes who had behaved badly ending up starving or dying of the cold or worse still being taken by the "demon fox avengers". These were ghostly foxes who were supposed to come and deal with foxes, or even cubs, who behaved particularly badly and who ignored the code of honour. Many modern foxes didn't believe in the demon avengers but those cubs who heard Slimlegs' terrifying tales generally concluded that they'd better not risk behaving too badly, just in case.

3. Don't attack children:

This was one which really surprised a number of the cubs; After all, in view of the fact that human beings were foxes' worst enemies and that they had few enough chances to hit back at them, surely attacking younger humans would be a good way of getting a bit of revenge?

However Slimlegs used to say that if foxes let children go there might be some chance, however remote, that humans might be prevailed upon to behave a bit better. As he put it to the amazement of some of the cubs "Even humans aren't all bad."

4. Never harry a pregnant cow:
Foxes used often have a bit of harmless fun barking at cows and getting themselves chased by these big silly animals, but Slimlegs enjoined them heartily to leave pregnant animals out of their fun.

5 Never steal from another fox, no matter how desperate your situation:

6 Never lie to another fox:
Foxes often found that they would tell white lies to other animals to get themselves out of a tricky situation, but it was strictly forbidden to lie to a fellow fox.

7. Never steal another fox's burrow:
Of all the crimes of Foxdom, taking another fox's burrow was considered the lowest. "Leave that sort of behaviour to the cuckoos" was Slimleg's advice.

8 Never interfere with Ballynahinch castle or it's immediate grounds:
This indeed seemed a very strange and archaic sort of rule. What possible reason could there be for obeying a rule like that?
Slimlegs however was again adamant on this point. This rule provoked some argument among the class, (the cubs were encouraged to participate in debate during the philosophy lessons), with some of the more radical cubs saying it was a classic example of how the code of honour was full of silly rules and really didn't make any sense at all. Slimlegs allowed this debate to go on for some time

and then he looked up into the night sky for a while and the moonlight could be seen illuminating his noble and learned features. He had quite a misty eyed look in his face when he looked down at the cubs again.

"Right" he said, "gather round and I'll tell you a story about the noblest human of them all".

All the cubs gathered round and waited in hushed silence for Slimlegs to begin his tale. Foxes, as I've already explained, love a good yarn and they all gather round in a small circle whenever a story is to be told.

Slimlegs told them a tale of Ireland in the long long ago, before living fox memory and long before that again when the greatest, the most noble and the kindest of all the human beings that had ever lived in Ireland or England or anywhere else for that matter had lived at Ballynahinch Castle.

This man, who had a funny name that the foxes couldn't pronounce, something like "Humbledrum Dick", had been a special friend of all animals and had done more for animals than any other man or woman before or since. It was rumoured that he could even talk to animals and Slimlegs had it on very good authority that there were at least two occasions when he had been seen talking to dogs and hares.

He had gone over to the mighty parliament in London (Freddie had a distant cousin who lived in London and he was most interested to hear Slimlegs talking about it) and he had persuaded them to set up special organisations to protect animals and to try to make sure that animals and humans would be better friends. Alas he had spent so much of his time in defending animals, and so little in looking after his own interests, that his enemies had eventually done him down and on his death his family had to leave the castle and never return.

Every year on the anniversary of his death the foxes and indeed many of the other animals who lived not too far from Ballynahinch had a special ceremony to mark his

passing and to give thanks for his life and to hope that one day perhaps another human would come who would love animals as much as he had done.
"You may find it hard to believe that a human could be kind to animals, but Humbledrum Dick was indeed such a man. I've often been around the grounds of Ballynahinch castle and I find them a very special place with a special kind of magic. Some day I think that the goodness of Humbledrum Dick may come back. It's very important that we foxes should be grateful and never abuse the grounds of the castle so that some day in the future maybe that goodness will come back." said Slimlegs.
The cubs listened in awed silence to this remarkable story and even though a lot of what Slimlegs said was above their heads they certainly enjoyed the story about the kindly human being even if they found it a bit hard to believe after some of the things they had seen.
Redeye in particular was sceptical about Slimlegs' story and indeed about the whole philosophy class.
"Kind human beings who can talk to animals indeed!" he would say. "I'll believe it when I see it."

These were some of the other rules taught in the philosophy classes:
9. Never , if you can help it, kill a full family of other animals:
Slimlegs felt that families were very important and that if a fox had had cause to kill several members of one family of, say mice or hares, that he should let the rest of them alone and even if he came across one of the same family when hungry he should let him go.
10 Never hunt on Christmas night.
Yes, it may come as something of a surprise to you that Christmas night is observed by foxes, or by the more old fashioned foxes at any rate, but when was the last time you came across a fox hunting on Christmas night?

Slimlegs explained that it was all to do with the notion of a time of "universal good will" and that if there was any chance that humans could be prevailed upon to be kind, then Christmas night was the time to do it.

11 Never make rabbit stew during the month of August:

This rather odd rule was one that Slimlegs never explained very well but he certainly stated that foxes disobeying this rule would go through awful suffering. While Slimlegs used to encourage a certain amount of debate he would often get tired of trying to explain everything and when some of the cheekier cubs like Redeye kept asking questions, he was liable to get quite impatient and say things like "Look, rules are rules and that's all there is to it. That's the problem with you young pups nowadays, never prepared to accept what your elders tell you!"

Calling cubs "pups" was usually guaranteed to put them in their place allright.

12 Always attend a fox confraternity when one is called:

Slimlegs made it clear that it was the duty of every fox to do his best to attend a fox confraternity if one was called and to contribute to the debates as best he could.

"Confraternities" which were used to discuss matters of interest to foxes and to talk about such things as changes to the rules of the code of honour or dividing up territories weren't called very often, and in fact no-one could remember for certain when the last one had been called, certainly not within living fox memory, so nobody thought this rule too important.

One evening after the classes were over and dinner had been eaten, the cubs were all gathered around in the dining room discussing the various subjects they had learned and which were their favourites. Freddie found much to his surprise that when he thought about it, his favourite subject of all was in fact philosophy. He wasn't sure why, and certainly most of the other cubs were bored stiff to the ends of their tails by philosophy and would much rather have been out hunting or tricking farmers than inside listening to dull old treatises on the rights and wrongs of fox behaviour.

His interest in philosophy didn't go unnoticed with the headmaster and when Freddie would give a good answer to a difficult problem or ask a particularly astute question, old Slimlegs would smile and say something like "Of all the cubs in this year's class Freddie is the one most likely to become a Renaissance Fox."

Freddie had no idea what was meant by this and thought it probably meant a fox who was good at catching wrens. It was only later that he learned that it meant a fox who was a good "all rounder".

What Freddie liked most about the philosophy class was the way it sort of connected things together. It gave you the feeling that if you behaved properly to other animals then they might behave properly to you, and every one would be much happier in the long run. Now Freddie wasn't one of these peculiar foxes who didn't like hunting; in fact there were very few of those , but he did come to believe that other animals, even humans should be given a fair chance.

What he didn't like about philosophy was the way in which it was taught, or taught by Slimlegs at any rate. There was too much emphasis on fear and the terrible things that would happen to a fox and indeed to all of Foxdom if foxes went about breaking the code of honour. Freddie indeed thought that all this sort of talk was the reason why a lot of the cubs didn't pay too much attention to the philosophy class.

One night, as class was over, Freddie was called aside by Dimplefleck and told to report to Slimlegs' office after dinner. Very few cubs had good reports about being called in by the Head, and Freddie thought that the wily old master had at last found out the truth about Fiona and the monocle. He paced around and around nervously for a good long time wondering what the Head had found out about his behaviour and hoping above hope that it wasn't as bad as he felt it probably was. Finally he said a quick prayer and plucked up the courage to make the long walk down to the headmaster's room. He couldn't think what he would say and he wondered whether the offence was serious enough to merit being expelled. It would be dreadful if he couldn't graduate now that he was so close to finishing the term and he dreaded having to face his parents if he were thrown out.

In fact much to Freddie's surprise when he showed up at the master's well appointed and comfortable apartment, he found that Slimlegs was all sweetness and light and he began to broach the subject of Freddie's later career. After some beating around the bush the headmaster finally got to the point.

Slimlegs used to wear a pair of half moon glasses. On special occasions such as hunt balls he would borrow Fiona's monocle, which he felt made him look particularly wise.

"I was wondering, young Freddie, if you had ever considered a career as a master of philosophy here at the academy?!"

Well! You could have knocked Freddie down with a flick of a horse's tail he was so taken aback! Now while Freddie had a certain admiration for Slimlegs, the thought of becoming a philosophy master and devoting himself to dusty years of study without the comfort of wife or family was one which he found quite frightening. He would have to think fast.
"Well actually headmaster" he stammered "I was rather hoping to start my own family and hunt for a few years, and in fact I think my parents are trying to make a match for me with one of the neighbouring young vixens back home." This of course was what in fox terminology was known as a bare tailed lie; arranged marriages had gone out of fashion years ago but Freddie thought that old Slimlegs would have approved of such old fashioned customs. He was right.
" I see, I see" said the old head " Yes perhaps it would be a good thing for you to have a family or two for a few years. But remember, if you ever feel the call of the academic life look me up and if I'm still alive I'll see if I can fix you up with a position. Now run along."
" Yes, headmaster, thank you headmaster, I'm very honoured headmaster, very honoured indeed" fawned Freddie and he backed away as quickly as he could without making his relief too obvious.
"Phew, that was a close one " he thought "better not tell this to any of the lads or I'll never hear the end of the farmering I'll get." "Farmering" was a term foxes used which would be the equivalent of our "ribbing" or "slagging". As you may have guessed foxes took a delight in making fools of farmers around the countryside and never lost an opportunity to make fun of them if they could.

Freddie's term at the academy was now almost over. Before completing his time however he had to go back with the rest of his class for a single day's refresher course in land hunting. This was to turn out to be an eventful day.

The cubs it should be pointed out were now coming to an age where they started to show an interest in the opposite sex. Freddie had rather a yen for Roundears but had not as yet been given any reason to believe that she felt the same way about him. (In fact Roundears did think Freddie ever so kind and cheerful, but she was still a bit shy about sending out the right signals).
Another pairing which had started off was that of Banshee and Prancer. They were both in different classes but as soon as class time was over they would meet up and start frolicking together in a way that some of the tougher cubs thought was right foolish. Nevertheless, everyone knew that once term was over, Prancer and Banshee would be off somewhere to start a family together.
Prancer was now in Freddie's group and set off with him, Fingal, Redeye, Roundears and the others on the refresher course on land hunting. This day mainly concerned the finer points of scent. For example they were taught how to tell how many animals were involved when they picked up a scent, how to tell whether a scent was fresh, how to pick scent up from the air and how to take wind speed into account. They were also taught about the various things to roll in , such as decaying leaves and dung (Yeuch), when you wanted to hide or disguise your own scent.

Towards the end of the session Fingal led the cubs out into an open windy area where they could pick up wind borne scents more easily, but while they were there he was very much on his guard stopping from the demonstrations every so often to sniff and listen in particular directions.
He was in the middle of explaining about the significance

of the scent of berries on a North wind when suddenly he stopped in mid sentence and turned sharply pricking up his ears and sniffing anxiously as he brought himself to his full height. After a moment he turned back to the cubs ;
"Quick, a pack of dogs and they're headed this way! Look sharp, gather yourselves up and back to the academy by the marsh beside the edge of Ballynahinch woods. Quickly now, but don't make any noise or they'll hear us."
The marsh they were headed for was about half a mile away and Fingal knew it would tighten them out to make it before the dogs were upon them. All the foxes and cubs were under strict instructions never to return directly to the academy if they were being chased but to go by one of the many pools or marshes that surrounded the academy. As well as protecting the other foxes at the academy it was always easier to lose your enemy if you went through watery ground, particularly if you knew the secret stepping stones which Fingal was well familiar with having set some of them out himself.
The trouble was however that cubs can't run as fast as dogs and they had quite a bit of ground to cover.
Suddenly they heard the bay of the lead hound. They were closer than Fingal had thought! The sound of the baying sent a shiver down Freddie's spine and made his furry coat stand on end.
One of the cubs at the front, Skylark I think it was, began to panic and broke off from the rest and ran ahead barking in fear or to keep his courage up.
"Quiet, quiet!" hissed Fingal, "they'll hear us ". But it was too late.
Having heard the sound, three dogs, an old sheep dog with one terrier and one mongrel lagging behind appeared over the brow of a hill not three hundred yards from the cubs and began to bound straight for them, baying madly, with another three coming about five seconds behind them again.

"Run lads , run for ye'er lives" shouted Fingal and all the cubs broke into a mad dash for the safety of the edge of the marsh.
Fingal anxiously tried to assess their chances; They were about two hundred yards over rough ground from the marsh now and the dogs were about three hundred yards behind them and gaining ; they might just make it but by God it would be close.
Fingal, though he could of course have outrun any of the cubs, stayed at the rear of the group to defend them to the death should anything happen.
As they came to within fifty yards of the marsh edge Fingal looked quickly over his shoulder. The dogs were about eighty yards behind them and having a bit of difficulty with the rough ground. "Yes" Fingal thought, "I think we'll just make it". Just then he heard a sharp cry immediately ahead of him and to the right. It was Prancer; his front paw had slipped into a hidden rock crevice. He picked himself up but he was limping badly. He was obviously hurt, possibly with a broken paw.
Fingal knew immediately that there was no hope of him making it to the marsh in time. Poor Prancer looked over his shoulder in terror at the approaching dogs who, rotters that they were, at once knew that he was the weakest and were making straight for him. "Run lads , run, don't wait for me" he said pluckily "I'll be allright , you'll see." The other cubs looked to Fingal.
"Quick , run for it " he barked, "I'll stay here and look after Prancer."
The cubs continued their dash to the marsh while Fingal, alone, turned to face the enemy.

The dogs as soon as they realised that they were going to be confronted, slowed down their running and three of them broke off to pick off Prancer while three of them began to square up to the gallant Fingal. This delay allowed the other cubs to make it to the edge of the

marsh. However they were not safe here as Fingal was the only one who knew the layout of the stepping stones that would lead them back to the academy, and without him the dogs would have a very good chance of picking them off one by one.
The cubs, not knowing which way to go, turned around to watch what was happening.
In the distance they could hear a high pitched yelp.

The lead dog was the old wiry looking sheep dog with one eye missing and one broken front tooth, both reminders of a fight he had previously had with a badger. The others followed his lead and Fingal immediately realised that if he had any chance of coming out alive it would be to go straight for Sheepdog at the earliest possible chance and hope that the others would take fright. Sheepdog however was a cunning old scrapper, who had been in many previous fights and was careful not to get himself into a position where Fingal could grab hold of him without the other dogs being able to come to his aid. He and his two companions, an Airedale and a mongrel hound, crept relentlessly closer to Fingal, the two seconds waiting for the moment when Sheepdog would pounce when they would also jump on Fingal leaving him no chance.
Prancer meantime was being surrounded by the other three dogs, one a terrier and two mongrels. Fingal had tried to cover Prancer's retreat but unfortunately had not been able to do so. Fingal snarled viciously at his assailants to let them know that if they were going to attack it was going to cost them dearly. Prancer too tried to snarl, but it came out more as a bleat. The dogs could see that he was injured and weak, and they began to close in on him. Just as a terrier was about to pounce on Prancer however Fingal dived straight at him and engaged in a mighty scrap. This left an opening for the other dogs to pounce and Sheepdog and his two followers

grabbed Fingal on the neck and leg. Fingal pulled and wriggled and was able to break free from one of the dogs and bit back but it was clear that he was fighting a losing battle. The two mongrels meantime had grabbed Prancer and began to pull at him from either side. The cubs looked on terrified; they could hear poor Prancer yelping in pain and terror, and though they would have loved to come to his aid they knew there was nothing they could do.

Just then however, they heard a rustling behind them and turned to see Fiona, Kelp Browntail, Mairteen, Zowie Fisher, and Slimlegs Whitepatch himself racing through the marsh. The high pitched yelp the cubs had heard earlier was Mairteen who, as luck would have it, was out on one of those solitary walks he used to take and had seen the difficulties Fingal's group were in from a distance. His special high pitched yelp was the red alert signal, and had brought the others rushing to his aid. They bounded straight out from the high grass and engaged the dogs in a vicious fight, forcing the two mongrels to let Prancer drop.

"Right", said Redeye as soon as they saw this, "let's go lads". Out the cubs charged, Redeye, Freddie, Roundears, Skylark, Browncap and the others, and grabbed Prancer by the soft part of the neck pulling him to the safety of the marsh as they had been taught to do in their escapology class.

In the meantime the foxes and dogs were fighting it out in a deathly pitched battle. Now however, the sides were a bit more evenly balanced.

Slimlegs, though no longer a young fox, had a lot of fighting experience behind him. He knew immediately that the best chance for the foxes was in attacking the leader of the dogs, and began to manoeuvre himself into a position where he could make an attack on Sheepdog who at that moment was shaping up to fight with Mairteen.

Slimlegs was grappling with a terrier and was more than a match for him. He worked his way over towards Sheepdog, and as soon as he got a moment, he went straight for the throat of old pack leader and bit as hard as he could. This was exactly what did the trick because Sheepdog realised that if he didn't get out fast his days were numbered. Slimlegs however would not let him go. With a mighty heave and quick tug the dog managed to toss Slimlegs away, but the headmaster, showing remarkable agility for a fox of his years, got straight up and dived with renewed vigour at his foe.
Sheepdog decided that he had had enough and instead of continuing the fight he turned on his heels and ran, with Slimlegs in hot pursuit!
When the other dogs saw this they began to lose heart and one by one they disengaged and ran off. The foxes had won, but only just!
A mighty cheer rang out from the cubs waiting at the edge of the marsh. Of the foxes, Fingal was bleeding and in fact had lost a large part of his tail. Forever after that he was to be known by his pupils as Fingal Halftail, but in one way the scars he bore were a sign of honour. Pleased though the foxes were with their great win, the delight of victory was short lived, for Prancer had been very badly injured and was bleeding from several wounds.

"Quick", said Slimlegs, "lets get him back to the hospital and see if we can save him." Zowie Fisher and Kelp Browntail between them put Prancer on their backs and padded back to the academy with the others following over the stepping stones through the marsh, panting with exhaustion as they went.

Foxes, like a lot of animals, have a habit of knowing when their loved ones are in trouble, even if the trouble happens far away. As soon as the party got back to the Academy, Banshee was waiting for them. She knew, as if instinctively, that something had happened to Prancer. All of the cubs had been left in the care of Briar Patch and were waiting anxiously at the gates of the main hall with Banshee to the front. As soon as she saw Kelp and Zowie Fisher coming with Prancer on their backs she ran straight up to them.

Prancer turned to her and said: "Don't worry, Banshee, I'll be allright", but Banshee could see that he was very seriously injured. They kissed each other tenderly in that very strange way that foxes have (if you have never seen foxes kissing each other they sort of rub the fronts of their necks together up and down a few times). By this time Slimlegs and the others had come back. Slimlegs and Fingal whispered among themselves looking occasionally at the cubs and particularly at Banshee.

"Right cubs, come along", said Slimlegs with his headmaster's air of authority in his voice, "the usual classes are cancelled for the rest of the day, I'll take you all for a philosophy class in the main hall. Briarpatch, Mairteen and Zowie will look after Prancer". Prancer smiled weakly at them as he was lead off to the sick bay. Foxes unfortunately do not have great medical techniques but they have methods of killing pain, such as licking the wounds of an injured fox and attempting to heal wounds with various leaves and berries, techniques the older foxes know about. Another method of treatment they have is a "cat scan" which involves treating the wounded areas with a cat's whiskers. Sometimes these techniques work but usually when a fox is badly injured the outlook is bad.

The cubs were led away by Slimlegs with Banshee looking anxiously looking over her shoulder. They were all seated around their various positions in the main hall while Slimlegs gave a lecture about the importance of helping a fellow fox, particularly a former pupil of the Academy, when he was in trouble. The cubs weren't paying great attention and were looking out of the corner of their eyes at Banshee who was sitting up near the front. Slimlegs was making a point in his lecture about the importance of giving assistance to younger foxes when suddenly Banshee got up on her four legs and let out a piteous, heartrending howl. At that moment all the cubs knew that poor Prancer was dead.

Foxes, like many animals, have a way of knowing when a mate or a loved one is dead. You may have noticed that some dogs suddenly leap up and cry when their master dies, even if it happens miles away.
Humans used to be able to do this as well, and some still can, though most humans have now lost this ability which animals still retain. Often in the middle of the night you may hear an animal crying painfully and you can usually be sure it is because their mate or one of their family has died.
All the cubs gathered around Banshee and tried to console her. "Don't worry Banshee, you'll get over it, you'll find another mate", said Slimlegs. "Time heals all things", he said, using a gentle tone of voice that the cubs had never heard him use before. Banshee could do nothing but yowl bitterly however. "At least", said Slimlegs, "he was able to see you before he died, not like a lot of foxes who die out in the open with no-one to help them".
That evening Banshee was given a special room to herself and at dinner all the foxes said prayers for Prancer. The academy had a very good record in not losing cubs and Prancer was the first cub to be lost in two terms. Slimlegs gave a very nice speech at dinner saying what a cheerful and gay young cub he had been. In the middle of the night however, Banshee's howling could be heard. Many foxes have a good way of naming their cubs and Freddie thought that Banshee had been well named for the sadness of her cry.

In the west of Ireland to this day many of the old people talk of the cry of the *banshee* when a loved one dies belonging to a family. This cry is a lonesome, sad whining, made it is said by a ghostly ancestor of the person who has died. It follows certain families and can be heard in the middle of the night rolling through the fields and the mountains and the valleys and whistling over the hills and through the forests. The cry of the Banshee could indeed be heard that night at the Vulpine Academy and caused many's the tear to fall from the eyes of the soft young cubs and even from the older eyes of one or two of the masters. Many people say that animals don't love each other the way humans can but any human that heard Banshee crying that night would not have said such a foolish thing.
Such, my dear children, is the sad life of a fox in the wild.

And what became of the dogs you might ask. Well they were ordinary household dogs and they went home that morning to their houses. One of the terriers was found by his owner pawing at the door with his tail between his legs. "Oscar", she said, scoldingly, "where have you been all night, you bad dog" and let him in as if he was the sweetest furriest little dog you ever saw. Children, keep your dogs locked up at night because as friendly as they can be when they are with you, they can be right blackguards if they get into a pack.

As Freddie fell asleep that day his thoughts weren't of philosophy or hunting or adventures, but of his poor friend Prancer, who would never be able to play with him again.

CHAPTER 4:

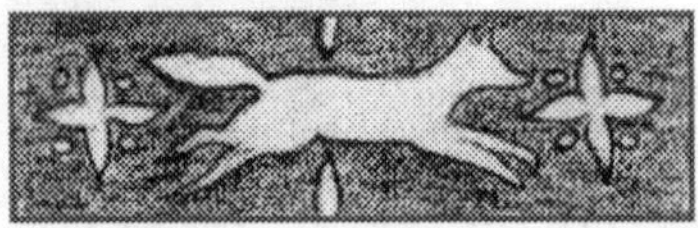

GRADUATION DAY AT THE ACADEMY

Graduation was due to take place some three days after Prancer's death. Foxes, like most animals that live in the wild, are able to get over their tragedies pretty quickly; they have to because they suffer a lot of tragedies.

Even Banshee began to pick up, and all the cubs were agog with excitement at the prospect of graduation. The list of successful candidates to be posted up in the great hall on the night before graduation was eagerly awaited and the cubs had great discussions among themselves about whose names would be included, who would get special honours and who, if any, would be kept back. When the great moment came, old Dimplefleck marched solemnly into the great hall ringing his silver bell with his list gripped firmly in his mouth.

Ignoring the entreaties of the excited and apprehensive cubs who quizzed him as to the results he silently pinned the list of results onto the large notice board in the great hall, and all the cubs gathered round searching for their names.

Freddie found, much to his surprise, that he had graduated with a *Magna cum yowla,* second Class. While he had been reasonably confident of passing he hadn't expected this great honour, and he put it down to his special interest in the philosophy class and the fact that the headmaster had something of a "furry paw' for him. (A furry paw in fox parlance is what we would probably call a "soft spot"). Freddie knew his parents would be delighted.

In fact , results at the academy were extremely good that year. There were a total of six *Magna cum yowlas* out of the forty eight students and only two of the cubs were indicated as not having graduated and were required to stay for an additional week's training in land hunting. Even these two moreover were allowed to take their diplomas with the remainder of the cubs so that their parents could come and enjoy the big day.

As Slimlegs said in his homily before dinner that night, graduation day was really a day for fox parents, and he enjoined all the cubs to be on their best behaviour and to appear properly groomed with clean and washed faces and looking their best for the following day. In view of the very good results he had been contacted by the editor of the *Galway and Mayo Foxly Chronicle* who was going to send out a "photographer". (Fox newspapers don't of course have photographs but what are known as "engravings of paw and brush" and the Chronicle's engraver, the well known Piers Huntingdon from the Wicklow mountains, was renowned for his accuracy and the pathos of his artistic effect. Pathos is something foxes very much appreciate!).

That night all the cubs paid special attention to grooming themselves and their friends so that they would look their best and the vixen cubs got to wear a special Academy ribbon in their tails. (Mortarboards, needless to say, were not allowed as they would be frightfully difficult to balance on a fox's head.) The *magna cum yowla* candidates however were given special blue robes with an opening at the back for their tails.

Freddie was looking forward to seeing his Mammy and Daddy again after the long six weeks at the Academy and when they met him they couldn't get over how much he had grown. At this stage Freddie was nearly as tall as his father. His mother of course was very weepy and his father pressed a pouch full of valuable duck feathers into his paw. Freddie had always found his father somewhat distant and it was only on great occasions like these that he would show his emotions. Nevertheless Freddie felt a lump rise to his throat as he could see the obvious pride in his father's eyes. "You're a fine looking young fox now, Freddie", said his father, " and I know that your education will stand you in great stead in the years to come".

Graduation took place in the great hall. Most of the parents, especially the simple country foxes, had never seen a room as magnificent as this before and they were hugely impressed with all the formality and the ceremony. The parents were lined up around the perimeter of the great circular room and Slimlegs and the other masters sat on the stage. Slimlegs had on a sort of black robe flowing down well past his legs and tail and, as if that wasn't bad enough, a most hideous looking red wig on his head.

The cubs, who were all in an ante room just to the side of the main stage, were all excitedly preening themselves and putting on their finishing touches. They were able to peep out to the main stage and when they saw the get-up of old Slimlegs it was all they could do not to burst out into howls of laughter.

All the parents however were very taken with the headmaster's splendour and had never seen anything quite like it before. The other masters also had their various special "trademarks" on display. Fiona, for example had her monocle and Fingal his bandaged tail while around his neck he wore a wolf's tooth, a valuable family heirloom which was the envy of the other fox masters. Kelp wore his waistcoat (now repaired) and Mairteen had on a hunting necklace made of duck bones and pieces of Connemara marble. Yes, the academy staff were certainly all out to put on a good show today.

The cubs were called in one by one and as each one entered the parents engaged in a light barking by way of applause. When Freddie was called in and the *Magna*

cum yowla was announced all the masters set up a screeching yowl into which the parents joined. Freddie could see his parents with tears glistening in their eyes. His diploma was a piece of oak tree branch about six inches long and about two inches thick with his grades marked there-on in fox language, and the paw mark of Slimlegs Whitepatch, signed with a great flourish. Some cubs don't attach too much importance to things like their diplomas from school, but many do: Freddie buried his in a special place and would often come back later in life and dig up his diploma and reminisce about his times in the academy. If you ever come across an oak branch about six inches long buried under the ground, look for the tell-tale scratches that may indicate that it is a diploma from a fox academy. If it is, put it back where you find it, as it may be a very special keepsake for some fox.
After he had received his diploma Freddie sat down in the main hall, being careful not to trip up on his blue robe in front of all those foxes as he went.
After the diplomas were all given out Slimlegs made his valedictory speech.
"Parents, you are all very welcome. Young cubs, or I suppose I should say young foxes now." (At this there was polite laughter from the audience; Slimlegs' speeches were never known for their great humour so the cubs felt it polite to laugh when it was expected). "You have all come to the end of a long and often difficult journey. You have learned here many of the skills that will help you to survive in the great world outside these walls. Equally importantly, in fact I think more importantly, you have learned the basics of the Fox Code of Honour and the fox rules of behaviour. Take these precious lessons with you as you go through life. You will often find yourself in trouble as the world and its cares press down on you, and we all know how difficult life has become for foxes in recent years. However, even in the most difficult circumstances, as you are being hunted and as you are

cold and hungry, take heart and think of higher things. Cast your mind back on some of the valuable lessons you have learned here so that in years to come you may be a proud, an honourable and a noble beast. If you can achieve that, your time in this academy and in this world will have been well spent."

Whitepatch's philosophy was that if you behaved well in this world, you would be rewarded in the next life, though he was never very specific about what kind of a life that would be.

After the speeches were over there was one more ceremony to be carried out called "nicking the ear". This was a passing out type of ceremony and even though it was largely symbolic, the masters attached great importance to it. A special fox called a Chaxer was brought all the way from Kilfenora in the Burren in Co. Clare to perform the ceremony which consisted in nicking or "chaxing" the ear of each cub before he formally graduated.

For the most part, the chaxing consisted of a very light little nip that you could hardly feel, though the cubs used to have great sport warning each other about how painful it was and telling tales of renowned and dreaded chaxers in the old days who would nearly take the ear off of you. All of the cubs seemed to be getting on splendidly with the chaxing but when Freddie' s turn came the chaxer, an old sly looking greybeard by the name of Rezing Rat, gave him a mighty nip such as to draw little spurts of blood! It was all Freddie could do to stop himself from yelping out loud in front of the entire crowd but as he looked up he could see the chaxer's face as impassive as if nothing had happened.

However, out of the corner of his eye he could see old Slimlegs Whitepatch with a wry smile on his face, and he felt that the nip had definitely been a special reminder to him, though he had no idea for what. The nip he had received left a small scar at the back of Freddie's right ear and years later many who came across him were to notice it. Though he was never to know it, that particular nick was to play a very important role at a crucial time later on in Freddie's life, and to come in very useful to him indeed.

Once all the ceremonies were over, the cubs and parents were given tea on the lawn just outside the great hall while Dimplefleck and Fingal kept watch. Even on great occasions like these, foxes had to be on the watch.
Then the time came for the cubs to say good-bye to all the friends they had made during their time at the academy, many of whom they might never see again, and of course to bid farewell to the masters with whom they had formed fond attachments. It was announced that there was going to be a reunion disco for the cubs in six weeks time but Freddie knew that not all of the cubs would be able to make it. He especially sought out Roundears and made her promise that she would be there. As you may have guessed Freddie was beginning to set his eye on Roundears, and he made a point of being very polite to her parents. Her father was a bit gruff but her mother, Merriweather Longtail, was quite taken by Freddie's polite and gallant charm and Freddie knew that he had made an ally there.
When saying good-bye to the masters Freddie made a special effort to seek out old Slimlegs, a master that the other cubs either avoided or only said very brief good-byes to. The crusty old head- master was very chuffed that Freddie had sought him out and even went so far as to rub necks with Freddie in a gesture of affection. As Freddie was going he said “Oh by the way Freddie, remember what I said about the philosophy mastership. If you change your mind just come and look me up.”
Then Freddie returned home with his Mammy and Daddy with many fond, and some sad, memories of the academy

in his head.

It was now early August and when Freddie got home he spent his days hunting with his father in the environs of his parents' burrow. His father was hugely impressed with Freddie's newly acquired hunting skills and the family were in no doubt that they would have plenty to eat that winter. Freddie was particularly concerned with storing up supplies for the cold weather, something squirrels are very good at. Of course most of a fox's diet can't be preserved for very long, but things like berries and nuts, even though none too tasty, can be stored up and if some pieces of meat are buried the right way underground they can be preserved for a time as well. Freddie and his father were also very keen on burying bones in various locations. Bones were a good source of calcium and could be a great stand-by in hard times.

Come September each year, with the cubs reared and food still reasonably plentiful, foxes tend to have a somewhat fallow period, and this is a time of year they devote to rest and relaxation. They like to visit each other's dens a lot and to engage in social activities such as playing cards, telling ghost stories, thinking up practical tricks to play on human beings, going to fox dances and generally getting ready for the mating season which usually takes place either side of Christmas.

The fox game of cards is played with dried leaves which are cut into particular shapes. This is why the game becomes popular in September when the leaves start falling off the trees. Various symbols are painted on the leaves and great excitement can be generated in the game with usually a prize like a chicken on offer after a night's play for the winner.

Cleverness and bluff are very important attributes to a fox and this may explain why cards are so popular among them. Card games were often known to lead to such

excitement that disputes would arise and sometimes foxes would throw down their cards and start snarling at one another. However if a fight would look like starting one of the older foxes would usually intervene to separate the fighting parties with some warning like "You'll have time enough for fighting when you meet the hounds of the hunt; save your fighting energies till then."
In truth foxes rarely end up fighting each other no matter how excited they get about cards or anything else. They often square up to one another with great shows of vicious-sounding snarling and barking, but usually they are glad of an excuse to back down.

Foxes, like most animals, and like a lot of people who live in the country, are very interested in the supernatural and love a good ghost story. Given their excellent sense of hearing they can pick up even very slight sounds in the middle of the night and they are very good (or so they think) at identifying ghost sounds. There are many stories told by the fox fraternity about foxes who were killed in the hunt coming back to haunt the master of the hunt and coming to wake him with bloodcurdling howls in the middle of the night.
One famous tale was of the vixen who was killed while out hunting and whose cubs starved to death because there was no-one to look after them. This vixen was said to be seen, as white as snow in December, roaming the hills around Corrofin in Co. Clare in the middle of the night, looking in burrows and out of the way places for her lost cubs. It was said that if this spirit, known as the White Vixen of Corrofin, ever called to a fox's burrow that it usually foretold a death in that fox's family, and Freddie's father claimed he knew one fox who had a visit in the middle of the night from the White Vixen, and that very night three of his cubs fell ill with the Scarletina and were dead within twenty four hours!
Another famous ghost story from Clare (a county

renowned for its ghosts), was tale of the infamous Black Ben, the Demon Fox of Feakle. He apparently had died fighting a group of fox hounds, but not before he had succeeded in killing three of them. As he died he is said to have uttered a curse that he would devour the heart of any dog that passed by that roadway for the following three hundred years.

Ben was as good as his word (or his bark in this case), and shortly after his death dogs began to meet untimely and horrible deaths on that road, many of them being found with looks of terror on their faces. It was only then that the curse that Black Ben had uttered was remembered.

The fame of this story soon spread far and wide and dogs who claimed not to be superstitious or who would never be afraid of a fox whether alive or dead, started coming to the road, a small by-road beside Biddy Early's cottage near Feakle, as a kind of a dare, or to show how brave they were. It was said that as many as came were found the following morning with their chests ripped open and their hearts missing ***and devoured***.

One dog renowned for his bravery, a black Alsatian known as Long Fang, tried the dare and managed to escape. When he emerged his coat had gone completely grey and he was never able to utter another bark. All he could do for the rest of his life was whimper incoherently.

The fame of these events soon spread far and wide, and soon no dog could be got to walk down that road for bones or money. If by chance a dog was out walking with his master and they happened to stray down this road, known amongst the dogs as the road of eternal night, the dog would freeze up like a block of solid concrete, break out into a cold sweat and refuse to move another inch. (Dogs are good at sensing these things apparently).

This part of the story was all very well, and gory though it was, most of the foxes thought Black Ben was doing well enough up to that point. However it was what happened next that really scared the tails off the foxes.

Apparently, once the dogs stopped coming, Black Ben, who had by this time become a Pooka, or a kind of demon, began to attack and devour the hearts of other animals ***including other foxes.*** One neighbour of Freddie's father, a very old fox, swore that when he was young and going to a dance one night in Clare with a group of his friends he had come across Black Ben;
"Instead of being red like a normal fox he was as black as the ace of spades and with eyes that weren't like any fox eyes I ever saw. They shone at you like burning coals and there was a look on his face as cruel as a human being. He was as tall as half an Ash tree and he came down at us from the sky like a kind of bat with a screech from him that came straight from the gates of hell!" (Foxes when they get to telling a story are prone to the bit of exaggeration).
Freddie's coat stood on end when he first heard this story and when he was on his way home with his father and a neighbour that night they would jump at alarm at every little sound they would hear. Indeed some foxes who would sit for hours listening to ghost stories would nearly be too frightened to go home on their own and would only go back to their own burrows if accompanied by some of their friends. Fox ghost stories are at their most popular during late September and right up to Halloween, which foxes always celebrate on the 16th of October in memory of Lilo Slimchance, the great fox leader and freedom fighter of the fifteenth century.

Another of the pastimes that foxes are fond of during September and indeed throughout the winter months is going to fox dances, or Hunt balls as they are often nicknamed with the kind of ironic humour which is typical of foxes. These are usually held in old deserted barns or tumble-down cottages rather than underground burrows because of the necessity of having some moonlight. If one group of foxes decided they were going to have a dance they would pick their location and leave various signals around, such as dance paw marks at recognised locations like trees at cross-roads or the gables of old buildings. (The way in which foxes can get messages to one another is quite elaborate and not fully understood by humans).

Foxes in a particular neighbourhood all have certain locations where they leave messages; messages relating to social events like dances or card games are usually left on the bark of Oak trees, and may consist of a daub or a series of scratches; messages relating to imminent danger are more often left on rocks beside drinking places such as streams or pools.

In any event word usually gets round quickly enough, as from September on foxes and vixens are on the look out for suitable mates. Music is usually provided by a few specialist foxes brought in for the occasion. The musicians howl in harmony while the others engage in the peculiar fox dance, which involves a slow rhythmic swaying between the dancing partners who usually have their necks touching and their heads pointing upwards to the heavens, with a sort of mock beatific look in their eyes. The howlers will sometimes be accompanied by a violin player, fox violins consisting usually of a piece of cat gut stretched over a young Ash branch. This is usually plucked, and though you or I would probably find the noise quite outrageous, it seems to be a great take with the foxes.

Admission to these ballrooms of romance usually costs about four duck feathers, or six if the musicians have a violin, and foxes are expected to bring their own refreshments.

As you may have gathered, feathers are the main source of currency among foxes, and while they can catch most of what they eat directly, they use the currency of feathers to buy in the little luxuries or for enjoyments. Feathers are quite valuable for foxes for lining dens and burrows during the Winter months, and a good bird hunting fox is usually very popular with the vixens!

Another activity that the more daring and the younger foxes get up to during the month of September is that of playing tricks on human beings, or "lamping" as they call it. If a fox succeeds in lamping a human being his fame will spread far and wide among his fellow foxes, and he will become hugely popular with a welcome before him at all burrows so that he can tell his story. Lamping, while it is good fun, is also a very dangerous business as it involves getting quite close to humans. However a successful lamper will usually be reckoned to be a daring and resourceful fox, qualities that are very useful in hunting and looking after a family, so a successful lamper will usually have no trouble attracting a mate. As luck would have it many farmers in the west of Ireland take their holiday in September, the same time as the All Ireland Fox Lamping championships are on, as this is the time of year when farmers are just finished the harvest and have a bit of spare cash.

Now farmers are a favourite target of the fox practical joke, largely because of the ongoing enmity between farmer and vulpine. One of the best opportunities for lamping is presented by the famous match-making festival at Lisdoonvarna in North Clare. This is a very ancient festival at which bachelor farmers from all over Ireland gather in the town of Lisdoonvarna during the month of September, with the aim of finding a wife.

Often for a farmer of a type not overly endowed with the social graces, the search for a wife may involve the consumption of large quantities of spirituous liquor, and this may leave him in a state of intoxication which lowers his resistance and leaves him easy prey to a good lamping by an astute fox.

For this reason Freddie and four of his friends, Redeye being one of them, decided, come the second week of

September after their graduation from the academy, that they would repair to the village of Lisdoonvarna in search of lampable candidates.

Their first night was spent in reconnoitring the village by prowling stealthily along the lane ways at about four in the morning, and it wasn't long till a suitable candidate presented himself.
Coming out of one of the hotels in the central square of the town they noticed a middle aged bachelor, in an advanced state of intoxication. As he was leaving, the owners of the hotel called him back and handed him a large baggy coat, of good quality wool and cashmere, which he had obviously left behind. He thanked them profusely with "Begod it wouldn't do to leave that behind. It was left to me by my late uncle, Dan Devitt, when he died last year. It was one of his most prized possessions. If I were to lose that coat I'd swear the ould fellah would come back to haunt me." and on he went on his way

Mr. Oscar Guilfoyle has a disturbing experience late at night at the Lisdoonvarna Match Making Festival.

walking on both sides of the street with none too steady a gait.

The foxes followed him closely taking the route in behind the street wall that runs from the town's main square to the spa well. When the mark, as the foxes called him, got half way down to the spa, the height of the wall was quite low and here he stopped to fill his pipe with some "baccy" and have a peaceful smoke. The night was quite warm and he put his coat, which he had been carrying, down on the wall as he filled his pipe.

Now, middle aged men who have had rather too much to drink are inclined to "drop off" and take forty winks, even when in a sitting position, (ask any barman) and it was just such an eventuality that Freddie and his companions were hoping for.

Sure enough, some time after the puffs of smoke had started billowing out from the pipe, the sound of a light snore could be heard and the mark's head began to drop. All the foxes knew immediately what to do. (Foxes often display this ability to be able to know what the other members of their group are up to without talking). Redeye and Freddie crept into either arm of the baggy overcoat while another one of the company, Blinky by name, kept a close eye on the mark.

When all was ready Blinky gave a very light tug to the victim's sleeve and the mark jerked his head back up. No sooner had he woken than Freddie and Redeye started standing up on their hind legs and swaying to and fro inside in the overcoat. This of course gave the impression that the coat had come to life. The mark stared in wide-eyed disbelief, unable to move with surprise and amazement. Just then Redeye poked his snout out from the neck of the overcoat and snarled with as evil a snarl as he could muster. At the same moment, the fourth member of the fox party, Lightpaw, a young vixen with a very silky tail, lightly rubbed her brush along the back of the victim's neck and Blinky let out one of those quiet,

high pitched fox screeches.
The mark was so terrified he nearly jumped clean out of his skin with fright. The pipe dropped out of his mouth and he ran off down towards the spa crying;
"Oh Holy God protect and save me! 'Tis the devil himself or else Dan Devitt come back to haunt me!! I knew I should never have taken that coat!! Help!! Help!!"
The foxes had a mighty laugh at this and were literally rolling around the ground with mirth. When they had finished they leaped up and clapped each other's front paws together and cried out "Lamped" to each other. This kind of play-acting was all the go in America apparently, and young foxes in Ireland thought it extremely "cool". Blinky ran and grabbed the pipe, thinking rightly that it might come in useful in the future.
The fun wasn't over just yet however, as the victim, a man by the name of Oscar Guilfoyle, had woken up half the town of Lisdoonvarna with his roaring and shouting. Windows began to open up along the Street with people enquiring what all the racket was about. The foxes took refuge in some tall Pampas grass (which gives excellent cover to a hiding fox) overlooking the scene from the front garden of a nearby hotel.
It wasn't long before Mr. Guilfoyle returned, accompanied by some tall burly men in black uniforms and peaked caps, with a trail of bystanders tagging along.
"I saw it as plain as day I tell you, inside in my own coat and with two huge horns on it......" (Presumably poor Redeye's admittedly pointy ears) " ....and horrible crooked fangs dripping with blood, and a hoof like a cow sticking out of the sleeve of my coat, and a face as ugly as the Hag of Beara....." (Here Redeye cocked up his head in indignation and it was all the other foxes could do to stop him going right out in front of all those people and growling)
"..........and he breathin' fire out of his nostrils, and a big long kind of pitchfork in one hand, and he touched me

right here on the back of the neck, and the screeching out of him was something horrible, and if it wasn't the devil of hell or the unfortunate soul of poor Dan Devitt that I saw then I'm not standing here this bright moonlit night!!"

Some of the bystanders were visibly frightened by this appalling tale but the men in black uniforms were having none of it.

"Come along now Mr. Guilfoyle, you've just had too much to drink. Now stop making all this disturbance! Move along now or you'll get a belt of me baton! Pick up your overcoat now and be on your way."

However no amount of threats or enticements could persuade Mr. Guilfoyle to lay a hand or anything else on his fine overcoat.

"I'll have nothing to do with that cursed coat ever again. And what's more I'll never drink another drop again as long as I live."

The men in black uniforms shrugged, but despite their bravery none of them seemed too anxious to touch the coat . At last however one of them took it and said he would dispose of it at "the station". Just as they were going, Mr. Guilfoyle noticed that his pipe was missing and began to look around suspiciously, but as the others were going he decided he would leave it and off he went.

This was undoubtedly one of the best lamps that Freddie was ever involved in, and as a result of it he and his group were awarded third place in the All Ireland Fox Lamping championship finals later that year.

Freddie and his friends had quite a few more exploits that week in Lisdoonvarna and I needn't tell you that Mr. Guilfoyle's pipe featured in more than one of them. After a week however the holidays were coming to a close and it was time for the young foxes to leave the pleasant town of Lisdoonvarna with all its fun and frolics and return to

their home base of Connemara.
After all, the year was getting on, and they would have to forget about lamping until next September and to turn their minds to the more serious business of finding a mate.

CHAPTER 5

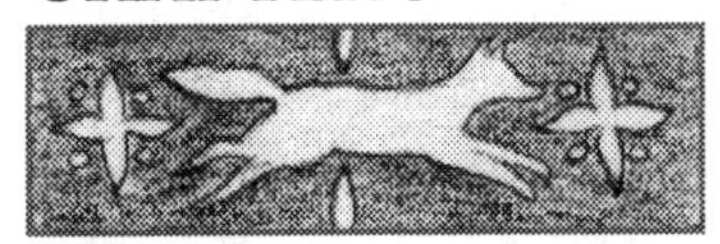

FREDDIE'S FAMILY

Come the beginning of winter, foxes both young and old begin the search for a partner. Now the thing about foxes that you may find hard to understand is that they often change their mate every year. They don't always do this, and some foxes stay with the same mate for all of their lives, and when foxes do change their mate it's not because they have fallen out with the first mate or because they want a new mate or because they're flighty, it's just the way foxes are. They may be perfectly happy with their present mate and may remain the best of friends with them and still not remain with them all their lives. Now if you can't understand this business about mates, it may be because you're a human and not a fox, and if you were a fox you would see nothing at all strange about it.

Anyway, about the October after Freddie's graduation his family were visited by his Auntie Silibert from Dublin and her two cubs Sylvester and Alexis. (Foxes from the East really do have such strange names!). Freddie's aunt Silibert was renowned as a match maker, and she was brought down to see if she could arrange a match for some of the local cubs, including, though he didn't realise it at the time, for Freddie.

Sylvester had gone to a school called the Foxrock business school, (Foxrock is a suburb in south Dublin), where cubs were taught all the latest scientific methods of survival, with a special emphasis on cuteness and slyness. Sylvester could be as sly as any fox when he wanted, but Freddie couldn't help feeling that he was a bit innocent about some things. He was a nice chap at heart, but he was inclined to put on airs and thought Freddie's description of the philosophy class was most "quaint " as he put it.

" It's every fox for himself where we come." he would say. "Survival of the fittest. And in a way that's a good thing. It may seem hard but in the long term it means that the fox species has a better chance of survival."

Freddie had to admit that there was a certain logic to what Sylvester said but he couldn't help feeling that "survival of the fittest" wouldn't be of great comfort to you if you were a less fit but more honourable fox.

"A lot of the older rules are considered a bit old hat now you know" said Sylvester. "we follow the teachings of fox leader Winston Drain, so called because of his ability to live in the most inhospitable of locations, even, it is rumoured, in a drain."

"Rats live in drains, foxes, or at least honourable foxes live in the wilds of Connemara" said Freddie leaving his superior cousin somewhat nonplussed.

Freddie was quite taken with his other cousin Alexis, in spite of her name which was very difficult for country foxes to pronounce. Alexis was turned out in the latest style and had her brush done up and coiffed so much that it looked almost twice the thickness of a normal fox's brush and very impressive. It certainly caught Freddie's eye!

Now unknown to Freddie, Silibert and Freddie's mother Gert had hatched a kind of plot between them that Freddie was to get hitched up with Alexis. It was thought that a country fox and a city vixen would combine the best of foxy wiles and that the cubs of such a union would be bound to be very clever and successful. It was also felt that if Freddie and Alexis tied the knot that Freddie would go to live in Dublin. Silibert was always going on about how the facilities there were so good and how you were never far away from a meal or a reasonably comfortable place to sleep and you would be amazed how much those wasteful humans used to throw out and all a fox had to do if he got into the right neighbourhood was to rifle through a few dustbins every morning and he could feed himself and even grow quite fat!

This business of foxes going to live in the city had taken off in great style in the previous twenty years or so and a lot of country foxes had made a great go of living in the city. Freddie would occasionally listen to his mother and aunt talking about the great things that were to be seen on the city and they would talk so much that it would quite wear you out listening to them, though they never seemed to tire of talking themselves. Freddie's father didn't have a great deal of time for Silibert and rows used sometimes start between them. More often though he used to keep his peace.

Freddie caught him out of the corner of his eye one time when the vixens were talking about the range of foodstuffs that were to be found in human dustbins, and he was looking into mid air with an air of sadness that Freddie had never seen before. Freddie thought how quiet he would sometimes be for a fox who was generally so active.

At any rate Freddie began to rise to the bait set by his aunt and his mother and began to take Alexis out walking, a procedure recognised in fox behaviour as preceding the beginning of a more serious relationship. Alexis was very self assured and used to entertain Freddie greatly with her tales of life in the city with its many excitements and strange sights that Freddie had never seen before. Interestingly Alexis didn't have such a bad opinion of human beings;

"They're not so bad really. One time when we were on the edge of a park some of the smaller ones came right up to us and started giving us bits of bread. I think they wanted one of us to come home with them and live in their house! I know of one fox who decided that he was going to find a human who would look after him and after watching a few families for a while he selected one and went right into their back garden and they started to feed him. In no time at all he was living full time in their back garden and he didn't have to do a thing all day except sit around and wait for the food to be left out."

Freddie found this story quite astonishing after all he had been taught in the academy about the unending cruelty of the human, and indeed after all he had witnessed himself.

"And what became of this fox after his time with the humans?" he asked.

"Well he certainly changed a lot" replied Alexis, "I met him about a year later and a fatter more prosperous looking fox I never saw! We tried to get him to come hunting or scavenging with us but he had no interest in the world in having any thing to do with us. He had gotten very lazy really. *"Tame"* is the expression I think he used. Still I suppose you can't have prosperity and a full belly and remain quite the same. I think it would be quite fun really living in a house and having your meals served up to you as if you were royalty."

Freddie found all this quite confusing. He had been taught at the academy that humans sometimes ensnared foxes with promises of a better life, but Slimlegs used to say that living with humans or getting too close to them was a fate worse than death itself, and that if a fox was faced with the choice of death or entrapment by humans that the only course open to an honourable fox was to choose death. However, the description Alexis gave of humans interacting with foxes wasn't too bad, even if it did appear that foxes lost a bit of their wildness in the process.

Freddie was becoming more and more taken with Alexis, and on their way home that night he snuggled up beside her and rubbed necks with her in the way that foxes do

before they start becoming serious about one another.
That evening as they got back they met with Sylvester who was carrying half a chicken in his mouth, the chicken already plucked and cooked.
"Where on earth did you get that ?" enquired Freddie, who guessed immediately that he had found it in some rubbish bin somewhere. Freddie didn't approve of rummaging in rubbish bins while there was good honest hunting to be had.
"I found it in a great place, some of the best rubbish I've ever seen actually." said Sylvester in a way that implied that he was quite surprised that there should be such good pickings in a remote place like Connemara. "A big old house on the far side of Ballynahinch lake there by..."
"Surely you don't mean Ballynahinch castle?" said Freddie aghast.
"Yes, I think that's what it was called, lots of choice leftovers. I was a bit surprised I didn't meet you there Freddie."
"It is strictly forbidden for any fox" said Freddie trying his best to keep his tone civil "to in any way violate the grounds of Ballynahinch castle. Surely even in Dublin you've heard of the Fox Code of Honour."
Much to Freddie's surprise he could see that Alexis did not take too kindly to this disparaging remark about Dublin and he felt that she was about to take her brother's side.
"Oh for goodness sake Freddie my dear cousin don't be so daft" said Sylvester. "Can you give me one good reason why a hungry fox shouldn't avail himself of the leavings of human beings? And don't give me any of that romantic old cods-wallop of yours about codes of honour."
Freddie was struggling to think of what the reason for staying away from Ballynahinch was and was just about to tell them the story about Humbledrum Dick when Alexis chimed in; "Yes Freddie you really are most charmingly old fashioned my dear boy" she said

coquetishly, "but you must try to keep up with changing times." and she padded off flicking her striking tail in the air and leaving Freddie downcast and lost for words.

That evening after dinner Freddie's father suddenly got up and said "Fancy a walk Freddie?" This was quite unusual for him as he usually took a nap after dinner and would only venture out for a game of cards or some story telling. When they were out walking Freddie's father began to talk about all kinds of strange things. About his life, and the various families he had had, and how a fox , even a simple un-educated country fox like him, would, if he lived to be a certain age develop a certain wisdom and a certain knowledge and an understanding of what his life was all about and of what would happen him after he was gone. He spoke more than Freddie had ever heard him speak before and Freddie suddenly realised that he was talking like this because he was dying.
Many older foxes who have gained wisdom have the ability to know when their time is up and they usually go off somewhere to die on their own in peace. Freddie had no idea how old his father was, and had never realised before that he was close to death. His father had had several families before he had met Freddie's mother, and this was the second family he had had with Gert. Freddie felt very sad and knew that even though he rarely spoke with him that he would miss his father. He sidled up close to him as a sign of affection, and he could see that his father was touched, even though he would never admit it. As they were getting back to the burrow his father asked "And how are you and that young wan, Alexis, getting on?"
"Very well", replied Freddie. "She really is very clever and I think she would make a very fine mate."
"Hhmmmmmh." said his father, deeply and slowly in a way that left Freddie in no doubt that he didn't think the match a good one.

A long, awkward silence followed.
"You know, Freddie," said his father at last, "I wouldn't like the upper lip of that particular lady. A bad upper lip is always a bad sign of a vixen, it can mean a shrewish temper." And with that he wouldn't say another word on the matter.
That sort of enigmatic comment was typical of foxes of Freddie's father's generation. They had a funny way of settling their opinion of another fox, and once their opinion was settled they rarely changed it.
Freddie was quite disappointed with his father's disapproval but decided that he wouldn't let it influence him too much. After all, he was practically a grown up fox and would have to make his own decisions. And anyway he thought Alexis' upper lip quite fetching.
The following day was the third day that Freddie and Alexis were walking out together. Usually if they walked out four days in a row a bargain of some sort would be sealed, and Silibert and Gert were very pleased with the way things were going. They would make such a lovely couple together, the two vixens used to say to one another.
As they were coming home that night Alexis suddenly sniffed something and rooting around in the ground she came across a very shallow rabbit warren with two baby rabbits. She immediately killed them before Freddie could stop her and started devouring them.
"Really Alexis," said Freddie, "they were only young babies. You know I think you are nearly as bad as your brother sometimes."
Though he was only speaking jokingly she reacted quite sharply.
"Don't speak about my brother like that, he's a clever and cunning fox and he doesn't have his head stuffed full of silly old fashioned ideas about codes of honour!" Her upper lip was trembling almost into a snarl and Freddie suddenly realised what his father had meant. Then she relaxed a bit.

"You'll have to buck up a bit when you come to live in Dublin you know" she said not unkindly.
Though this last comment was meant as a peace offering it had the reverse effect on Freddie who was frankly appalled at the forward nature of what she had said. How could she take him for granted in that way when nothing was settled between them?
The scales were beginning to fall pretty rapidly from Freddie's eyes. The two young foxes padded home in silence and just as they were reaching the den Freddie spotted the ears of a cow just over a nearby ditch. He sniffed the air and counted what day it was and then a brief smile of remembrance flashed across his face.

That night Freddie decided that the time had come to act. He of course could not behave dishonourably so he felt that he must not walk out with Alexis the following fourth day. He had decided that Alexis, with all her charms, her fine tail , and her delightful swagger was not the vixen for him. He took her aside that evening after dinner and told her that he would not be walking out with her the following day. Nothing more. He didn't want to get into a scene. (Foxes despite their love of drama and story telling are not great ones for the emotional scenes). Alexis took this in good part, and Freddie felt that perhaps she was coming to the same conclusion herself. Anyway, he knew that she would have no trouble finding a suitable mate, either one of the local foxes who wanted to go to Dublin or one of her own city slicker types when she got back home.
Freddie began to realise now that a lot of his Aunt's manoeuvring over the previous few days had been aimed at a particular end and he knew that he would have to put the matter beyond doubt in her mind as well. At about midnight he got up and announced that he was off to the Academy re-union disco. Just as his aunt was about to suggest that Alexis could go with him he said, "I

have a date with an old flame of mine, a young vixen by the name of Roundears Merriweather."

I need hardly tell you that you could have knocked Gert and Silibert over with a single flap from a duck's wing! Freddie's mother glared sharply at him and he began to wonder if he had handled this rather delicate family situation a bit too abruptly.

"But Freddie......." his mother began, pleasantly enough but with a distinct edge to her voice.

"I think Freddie is old enough at this stage of his life to decide who he wants to take to a disco without help from his mother."

It was Alexis, and Freddie smiled at her gratefully for her help.

This surprise intervention left Gert and Silibert for once stumped for words, and Freddie took his leave.

As he sauntered towards the door Freddie's father, who had been sitting reading the paper and who never involved himself in family disputes unless things looked like coming to bites, winked at him out of the corner of his eye.

This was all very well thought Freddie, as he faced out into the cool night air and pointed himself towards the disco. He had overcome one problem, now for another. He had, he realised fully, been guilty of exactly the same thing as Alexis earlier on that day; he had taken Roundears for granted.

How did he know but that she hadn't already found a mate? Even if she hadn't he had only the remotest idea that she would take to him. He would look a right rabbit (this was an expression foxes used for describing foolishness or having done something badly or without finesse), if after mentioning Roundears in a manner which every one understood to be matrimonial, he was now to fail to attract her.

"Still, nothing for it Freddie" he thought to himself, "into the valley of the hunt rode the sixty brave foxes!" (This was a line from a poem about how sixty foxes had once succeeded in routing the North Mayo hunt in days of yore, and Freddie had often heard the older foxes reciting it to themselves when they needed to pluck up a bit of courage).

The disco was held in an old thatched cottage about a mile from the academy on the edge of Ballynahinch lake, and with a splendid romantic view towards Ballynahinch castle. It was an ideal venue in that half of the roof was off and it let in lots of moonlight while if it rained there was always the other half roof to provide shelter.

Freddie could hear the howling as he approached and it was clear that the night's activities were in full swing.

Discos were all the latest rage at that time. They were very similar to dances really except that instead of fox violins there would usually be a concentration on two groups of howlers in harmony and there might, as in this

Rock 'n' Yowl had become very popular among the young foxes of Connemara, and was all the go during the September disco season.

case, be some professional dancers on the stage. All of this was provided for by the academy as a sort of treat to their past pupils and to help them to find a mate. This disco was regarded by many as a very important social occasion, more like a ball really, and a lot of the foxes were turned out in their best finery.
Fiona and Fingal were both there trying to oil the wheels of romance and they were encouraging the shyer foxes to ask the vixens out for a dance.
When Freddie arrived all his old friends came up to say a few barks to him and while he was busy exchanging pleasantries in this way he was looking out to see if he could see any sign of Roundears. At first he couldn't, and then suddenly he caught her out of the corner of his eye dancing with the notorious Burgo De Longtail, a distant cousin of hers and a fox who had a fearsome reputation as a breaker of vixen hearts! Burgo was a past pupil of the academy who showed up at the disco every term. He tried to convince all of the vixens that he was only three years old and because of his good looks and somewhat vulgar charm many of them believed him. However it was rumoured that he was nearer six years old (positively late middle aged in fox terms) and that he used to dye his whiskers a splendid red with an elderberry juice concoction of his own.

Freddie was, to say the least, perturbed, and he realised that the situation called for pretty quick action.
He tried his best to catch Roundears' eye but unfortunately she and Burgo were in the middle of a slow dance and they both had their eyes pointed heavenward in that somewhat exaggerated pose that foxes use when dancing. If this level of intimacy kept up, Freddie thought, it might be too late for him to do anything. Looking around for inspiration he spotted a friend of his mother's who was one of the singers on the stage and a plot began to take shape in his mind.

He managed to whisper into the ear of his mother's friend to make sure that the next song was a good lively rock and yowl one with lots of quick steps that would prevent too much bodily contact. This, thought Freddie, would interrupt Burgo's amorous advances a bit.

As soon as the rock and yowl number came on he could see Burgo looking around suspiciously to see who was responsible for ruining his bit of romance at such a crucial moment. As it happened Burgo had himself used this trick on one previous occasion against a rival fox and he was in no mood to have it used against himself tonight. Now Burgo, for all his good looks, was getting a bit long in the fang, and a life of dissolute conduct and intemperate behaviour had left him some-what less trim than a fox of his years should have been. The upshot of this was that while Roundears took to the rock and yowl in great style and was leaping around the floor like a two month old cub, Burgo began to get a little bit puffed and to pant fairly heavily. We all of course know that foxes don't sweat, but rather pant to get rid of their excess moisture, and the result of Burgo's panting was that a large amount of moisture began to collect in the region of his whiskers.

Freddie kept the pressure up with his friend at the stage ensuring there was no let up to the rave type music and eventually he saw that his plan was beginning to bear fruit. ***Burgo's whisker dye was beginning to run,*** and Freddie could see a small fleck of grey showing through. Freddie knew that he would have to act quickly, as a fox of Burgo's years and cunning wouldn't be that easy to outsmart. He grabbed the nearest vixen, hardly giving her time to reply to his invitation to dance, and sailed over with her in the direction of Roundears and the panting Burgo. Just as he got to them he got hold of his vixen and executed a wild kind of a twirl that brought him colliding straight into Burgo and sent all three of them sprawling tails over ears. As they were falling

Freddie made sure he rubbed his shoulder off the edge of his rival's whiskers to smear as much dye as possible.
"Why you impudent young pup" roared Burgo as he picked himself up " Why, I'll... ,I'll pick you up and shake you like a rat!! I'll, I'll ...." Just then he was interrupted by the sound of a brittle, vixen-like tittering. It was Roundears.
"Why Burgo", she laughed , "your...., your whiskers , they've gone all grey."
Burgo put his paws to his face and immediately realised what had happened. He was about to make an attack on Freddie (and he had a lot of fighting experience) but a number of the other foxes were gathering round and beginning to smirk at his whiskers. He felt under the circumstance that if he was to retain any reputation as a fox Romeo he had better leave quickly before word of this embarrassment spread. Muttering his excuses as gallantly as he could and covering his whiskers with a handkerchief he left hurriedly.
Freddie's dancing partner in the meantime had stormed off muttering "Never been so insulted in my life! That wretched fox can't dance a step. About as much sense of rhythm as a mating hedgehog. Why he practically dragged me all over the floor and stood on my front paws twice!"
When Roundears saw Freddie he could swear he saw her eyes light up and then she looked down shyly.
"Why Roundears, how wonderful to see you."said Freddie feigning surprise. "Ahm........., would you like to dance."
"Why, yes Freddie," she replied, "I'd love to."
"I,...I hope I haven't interrupted you?"
"Not at all." smiled Roundears sweetly, "I was rather hoping that I would find some excuse to get away from our middle aged friend. I mean, he is a pleasant enough sort of fox but who does he think he's fooling with his elderberry dye?"
"Hmm." thought Freddie to himself "There's more to this

lady than a nice pair of roundy ears!"
Freddie's friend on stage had been watching proceedings and arranged that the next three sets (each consisting of three songs) were all slow and "furry" as foxes called romantic songs, and before long both Freddie and Roundears were gazing sweetly into each others eyes.
Freddie waited for a lull in the music and then he asked Roundears out for a stroll in the moonlight. (He wasn't too experienced with the vixens when it came to romance and even though he knew this sounded a bit corny it was the best he could think of).
He needn't have worried however about impressing Roundears with sophistication or tall tales of exotic adventures or of hunting exploits the way a lot of young foxes do when trying to impress a vixen to whom they have taken a fancy. He found that he and Roundears could chat away to each other about almost anything as if they had known each other for years and years, and even when they were silent it didn't seem awkward.
Soon they were talking to each other about the things that mattered to them; their hopes for the future, philosophy (that mattered to Freddie at least), nice places to live, how beautiful moonlight could be on a crisp Winter's night, and before the disco was over Freddie had asked Roundears to be his mate and she, without a moment's hesitation, had agreed.
Freddie went home skippingly that night , stopping every so often and tossing his hind legs up in the air and clicking his back heels together as his legs came down.
By Jingo he had done it and he was the happiest fox in all of Connemara ! Roundears had agreed! She had gone home to tell her family and would show up at Freddie's family burrow in two days time!

Next day he told his family that he had made his match. It was the custom in that part of Connemara for new vixen brides to join the family of their mate until they "dispersed" around November or December. Freddie's mother was a bit taken aback by the suddenness of it all and was a trifle miffed that she had not been in some way "in on" the match, (She was notorious for having arranged, often without their knowing, the matches of most of the children of her many families), but she couldn't help being infected by Freddie's excitement and in no time she was quizzing Freddie about what Roundears was like and asking him to tell her the story of how he had won her from that disreputable Burgo de Longtail. She laughed heartily every time she heard that tale and she repeated it several times to her friends.

Foxes, despite their love of drama and show, rarely make a big to-do about getting married. Perhaps it is because their married lives can be short and they may lose their mate fairly quickly, either to death or misadventure. However when Roundears did arrive Gert had the burrow looking spick and span and served everyone an elaborate meal consisting of Rabbit pie, oysters, quail's eggs and a main course of stuffed imported porcupine no less. Dessert, for those who could find room for it, consisted of wild honeycomb with blackberries and Larks' tongues. All of Freddie's immediate family who were invited to meet the new bride declared that they had never had a feast quite like it before.

That November Freddie and Roundears moved out to their own burrow , about three miles distant from his parents to a site on the far side of Ballynahinch lake. They were very lucky in that they found a site right under an old Oak tree which had previously been occupied by a large family of badgers. The badger family had decided to move to the county of Leitrim where a lot of new trees were being planted and which was considered something of a land of opportunity among many Irish wild creatures. An aunt of Freddie's had seen them depart and had sent word to Gert that if the newlyweds came quickly they could have it.

Oak tree burrows are very prized because of the great stability they gave and also because Oak trees tended to attract lots of other animals and birds such as squirrels and magpies who could become useful prey during hard times.

Oaks were becoming quite rare in Connemara so Freddie and Roundears considered themselves pretty lucky. Freddie immediately set about renovating and improving his new home and soon the pair had transformed it into a virtual palace.

Of course they had some other temporary burrows as well for when they were out hunting, but the oak tree burrow was their main home where they would spend many happy days.

Roundears had a particularly dainty paw when it came to interior decor and even though they had few of the luxuries such as duck feather quilts and blankets, their burrow had a very individual look to it that was commented on by all who came to visit.

Freddie had by now become a very good hunter, and what he lacked in experience he certainly made up for in speed and fitness, and that first winter he and Roundears had no shortage of food and could afford to devote time to the finer things in life such as making quilts, meeting and discussing the great events of the day with their fellow foxes and walking together beside Ballynahinch lake.

Freddie often tried to persuade some of his friends to engage in team hunting to develop their skills. However while food was plentiful, as it was that winter, he found that few of his fellows were too interested and only rarely did he succeed in organising a team. Freddie felt this a great pity as he enjoyed the company of other foxes in a hunting expedition and he felt that when a harder winter came, as come it surely would, that team skills would be very useful for all of them.

Sometimes, when they were alone and thought nobody was watching, Freddie and Roundears would dance by the light of the moon.

There was no snow that winter and Freddie and Roundears passed the time without any great hardship, resting a lot of the time. Freddie felt wonderfully refreshed when Spring came and was amazed at how things changed so quickly come mid February; the buds were coming on the trees and the birds were beginning to come back and everything looked pleasant and hopeful. It was really very good to be alive he thought. There were changes in Roundears too as it was now time for her to have her first litter of cubs! Freddie and Roundears were hugely excited at the prospect of having their first family. When the time came Roundears went to the warmest part of the burrow and Freddie covered her with leaves and what few feathers they had collected. It was a difficult birth and took quite a few hours but eventually Roundears gave birth to four beautiful cubs, three dog foxes and a vixen, who were christened Foxglove, Ringtail, Ratcatcher and Henry. (Henry was called after Freddie's father). Rather unusual names you might think but then as you may have gathered from the story so far, Roundears had a somewhat individual and stubborn streak and despite Freddie's best endeavours she got her way with the names. The grandparents were invited over to see the new cubs and were delighted with them, though Roundears mother threw her eyes up to heaven when she heard the names as much as to say "Will that daughter of mine never get sense?"

Freddie was alarmed to see the deterioration in his father during this visit. He was now definitely an old fox and Freddie felt that he would not last to see the next Summer.

He was right. About three weeks later Freddie's father decided that the time had come for him to go. He kissed his wife of two families, Freddie's mother Gert, said good-bye and disappeared into the depths of Ballynahinch woods to die. He didn't want to make a fuss for anyone and he found a quiet shallow hole in the base of an old Ash tree and there laid down his head for his final sleep. A lot of foxes do things this way and they don't seem to need any one with them when they die. It is of course a sad way to go from our point of view but it is the way foxes prefer to spend their last moments, alone with their thoughts.

Freddie's father remembered many things on his last night in the world. He was over ten years old, which is pretty old for a fox I can tell you. He had had a hard enough life, especially in his younger years when he didn't have a lot of hunting experience. That was why he had tried to send a few of his cubs from his later families to a good school so that they could get a bit of a start in life and not always be under pressure. He had seen two of his four mates die, one from poison and another killed by dogs. That memory still caused him pain when he thought about it. He had been lucky on more than one occasion in being able to escape the traps and the poison that humans were becoming more and more expert in, and he considered himself very lucky indeed that he had lived so long and that he was able to die in some peace rather than on a cruel trap or with dogs bearing down on him.

Foxes don't think very much when they are alive about what the future holds, after all there' s not much point when you don't know from day to day whether there will in fact be a future, but funnily enough when they come to die they do tend to think about the future for their families and indeed for the whole extended family of Foxdom.

He remembered hearing something about this from an old travelling philosophy fox whose favourite saying was that something had to die before it could live. Freddie's father had no idea what this meant before the last few moments of his life, but now he began to think about the future for all foxes, about how difficult things had become for foxes even in the time since he had been a cub, and he began to understand for the first time how important were things like the code of honour, and fair play for other animals , even though he had broken these rules on more than his fair share of occasions during his long life. He began to think of the many cubs to whom he had been a father over the years; He found it hard to recall them all and he knew that he had been a better father to some than to others, but he felt he had improved as time went on.

One of his favourites of the thirty or so cubs he had helped to rear had been Freddie from his last family, and he was happy to think of him settled in a good burrow with a good mate. Yes, he thought , Freddie was the kind of a fox who could well make his mark in the world.

Such were the thoughts of Freddie's father as he became sleepier and sleepier and slid gradually into what foxes call "the great change".

Far away, over the peak of Benbaun mountain, over the purple heather that clothes the side of the majestic slopes of Connemara, over the gently lapping waters of Ballynahinch lake, under the base of a mighty oak tree, Freddie and his family were fast asleep. Freddie suddenly woke up and a feeling of great sadness came over him. He was perplexed for a moment but soon he knew that he had lost a friend and protector. It was as if a cool wind had come and touched him on the back of the neck, (a place foxes really don't like being touched), and even though he was sad he felt slightly comforted as well. He went outside to look at the declining light over Ballynahinch lake. Roundears, who had noticed him waking up was going to go with him but then she understood that it might be better to leave him alone. The cubs slept soundly.

That Spring Freddie was kept busy foraging and hunting for the four hungry mouths that had arrived, but he had stored some bones and other supplies from the previous winter and he didn't find it too difficult to make ends meet. About a month after the birth Roundears was able to accompany him on short forays and soon they had built up a little stockpile of basic foods like rats and squirrels so that they could devote some time to hunting the more difficult prey such as ducks. After about another month the cubs were able to go with them on some trips and Freddie was able to teach them some hunting and survival skills. Unfortunately, as this was their first family, Freddie and Roundears were not able to afford the fees to send any of the cubs to the academy, but with what both of them had learned themselves, they were able to give all their charges a pretty good home education.
Ratcatcher in particular showed promise as a hunter and was very soon into pouncing and fishing in great style. Henry and Ringtail learned a lot from Ratcatcher who was undoubtedly the leader of their family group. Foxglove was a somewhat shy and thoughtful young vixen cub, but she was pretty clever for all that and one day amazed Freddie with the cunning she showed in trapping a pigmy shrew at the river's edge. Freddie never

ceased to be astonished at how different in personality the four cubs were and the different interests they showed almost from birth.

Freddie had a good deal to do in his first Spring making sure that his territory was well marked out. Foxes won't normally invade the territory of another fox but it's very important to ensure that your area is well marked out with proper scent and markings if you want to avoid a nasty dispute that might end up in fox court, a very tedious and expensive procedure. Freddie enjoyed showing his cubs the basics of marking out territory and he got great enjoyment from their company. He would miss them when the time came for them to disperse. Fox cubs usually promise to keep in touch after dispersing, but Freddie knew that it wasn't always possible for them to do so. It is said that a fox always feels a special attachment to his first family and to his last family, and even while Freddie was teaching his cubs the skills they would need to stay alive in the big bad world, he was thinking of the day when they would leave the family home and he might never see them again.

Ah well, no point in being gloomy thought Freddie, better enjoy their company while they're here. In any event the fox holidays of September would soon be coming round again and then all of the foxes could have some fun and take their minds off weightier matters.

However, events were to happen later in that year that would altogether change Freddie's and Roundears' plans for that Autumn, and indeed have an effect on the remainder of their lives.

CHAPTER 6

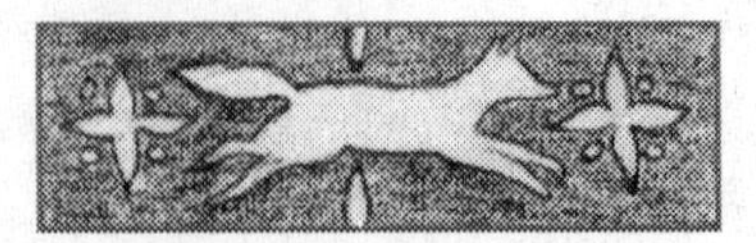

THE LEADER OF ALL THE FOXES.

About the middle of July of the year of Freddie's first family news reached the foxes around Ballynahinch which filled them all with great sadness. The leader of all the foxes, known as the greatest fox in Ireland, had died. I haven't told you about the leader of all the foxes up to this because it really didn't affect the story of our hero too much.

The foxes in Ireland used to pick a leader who would be chosen by special fox electors. These were foxes who had reached a certain standing among their fellows, and the practice of having electors was an ancient custom going back so far that no fox could remember exactly when it had started. To become an elector a fox had to have achieved a distinction of some kind such as having won the All Ireland lamping championships or having gotten the better of human beings in some particularly clever way.

The Leader Of All The Foxes was elected for life, and in former days he used to enjoy a great deal of power and prestige and could make all kinds of decisions concerning how foxes were to behave towards one another, interpreting the fox code of honour, settling territorial disputes, deciding which groups of foxes would leave an area if it became overcrowded etc. etc., and the leader's word was always strictly followed.

In more recent years however, with the fox code of honour falling into disuse a bit, foxes began to pay less attention to the leader's pronouncements and tended to settle disputes among themselves (often with consequences which were less than happy), and the role of the leader began to be seen as being largely ceremonial. Indeed many foxes began to wonder openly whether there was any point in having a leader at all.

Freddie remembered old Slimlegs always insisting however that the role of the fox leader was all important, and saying that if the foxes ever stopped having a leader that the whole fox brotherhood would be in for dire trouble indeed. Nevertheless many of the foxes, particularly the city foxes, began to think that the whole business of the leadership and the way it was run could

Clarion was a very humourous and pleasant fox by nature, but often the cares of his high office weighed upon him.

do with a good shaking up. The last leader hadn't helped matters much. He had been there for ages and ages and he hadn't seemed to do anything new or remarkable during his time.

Freddie was surprised however that many foxes, particularly those of the older generation were very saddened when he died and special ceremonies were held to mark his passing.

Great speculation then ensued as to who would be the next leader, with several notable contenders being hotly tipped. Some foxes wanted to see a fox who would sweep vigorously with a new brush and introduce some reforms into the code of honour. Others wanted things to continue the way they were. When the new leader was eventually elected he seemed to satisfy no-one. He was a small elderly fox with a mischievous twinkle in his eye by the name of of Carillon, or Clarion as he was more commonly known, and he appeared to be something of a compromise candidate.

However, much to everyone's surprise Clarion turned out to be as good as his name implied, and set about a vigorous programme of work, introducing quite a new style of leadership and getting rid of a lot of the old complicated rules and regulations that used to surround the workings of the leader's inner circle. A lot of his advisers tried to slow him down a bit but Clarion was having none of it. For example he introduced a much accelerated method of settling territorial disputes which drastically reduced legal fees, (needless to say this didn't make him too popular with the vulpine lawyers), and in no time at all Clarion had become one of the most popular leaders of his time.

The real surprise came however in only the second month of his term of office when Clarion announced that a Fox Confraternity would be held to look into the whole issue of the code of honour and how it was to continue in operation.

For a lot of older foxes this came as something of a shock; after all the code of honour had existed for longer than anyone could remember; having changes made to it was something they thought would never happen.

A foxes' confraternity is of course an extremely rare event. No-one could remember for certain when the last confraternity had been held and nobody was quite sure what decisions it had reached even though they were all sure it was written down on a piece of paper and kept somewhere at the Fox leader's arch burrow.

Foxes were generally aware of the rule in the code of honour which stated that they were supposed to make their best effort to attend a fox confraternity when it was held, but as they all knew this was very unlikely to happen it was not something they thought about much. I needn't tell you that many foxes including Freddie were quite surprised at the notion of the code of honour being changed or even deleted, and grumblings of discontent began to grow as to whether the new leader had in fact over-stepped the mark a bit despite his undoubted popularity.

That late August the news of the confraternity spread like wild fire throughout the foxes of Ireland and it was the main talking point at the usual round of meetings, dances and card games which began to be held in September. Even the younger more sophisticated foxes who claimed to have little or no interest in the code of honour couldn't help but be caught up in the excitement about the big changes that were going on.

Clarion sent word that the confraternity was to be held during the first and second week of October; this would ensure that cubs would be reasonably well reared and wouldn't be too difficult to look after. The confraternity was to be held in the ancient underground warren of Clonoulty underneath the Phoenix Park on the west of Dublin city. This was seen as a very clever move by Clarion and as being highly symbolic. Clonoulty being an ancient seat of Irish fox learning would clearly give the impression that the confraternity was in the tradition of upholding the basic precepts of the code of honour. However the fact that it was held in the city of Dublin would also acknowledge the rising importance of the urban fox.

Most foxes had to admit they were pretty pleased with the choice of venue. If nothing else they had to acknowledge Clarion's wily nature. (Wiliness you will understand is something which foxes hold in very high regard indeed). Clarion also sent word that it wasn't necessary for every fox to attend the confraternity but that those who wanted would of course be welcome and that every family or extended family should try to send one member. This ruling was seen as a very sensible reform and won the approval of all but the crustiest and most old fashioned of foxes. Previously fox leaders would never have bothered much about the convenience of lesser foxes, and it was this thoughtfulness that endeared Clarion to the ordinary "fox in the field".

Of all the foxes in the area around Ballynahinch lake, Freddie was the one who was probably most interested in the confraternity. Roundears also was very interested and when the matter was discussed with their immediate family and friends they decided that both Freddie and Roundears would go as representatives of the family and the immediate area. Redeye, who lived about a mile and a half away, had no interest in the world in going, thinking that the whole thing would be very troublesome; "Will the confraternity put rabbits or rats on my table?" he would ask.
Freddie answered him that it might well do but he didn't bother getting into a heated debate as he knew that at heart Redeye was a good fox and a reliable friend.

Rat Catcher was now almost a fully grown fox and it was decided that he would take charge of the other three until Roundears and Freddie returned in mid October. Much to Freddie's surprise Gert was very interested in the whole business of the confraternity and while she reluctantly decided that she wouldn't go because the journey to Dublin was such a long one, she asked Freddie to take very careful notes and to tell her everything that happened when he came back.

Freddie and Roundears then began to make preparations for their long journey. Foxes, as you may know, have a network of well travelled routes which criss-cross the whole countryside of Ireland. These are very different routes from the roads that you or I would take. They involve going along river beds, over mountain ridges and along ancient bog roads. These fox highways as they are known, are usually pretty safe and contain a lot of identifiable landmarks which are very important to enable foxes to find their way. Many of the more daring foxes who have a long journey to make and who don't want to walk all the way try to stow away in the backs of trucks or railway carriages. Foxes who stow away in trucks have been known to end up in a totally different location to their original destination and have often been stranded with no idea of where they had finally ended up. For that reason trains are generally considered a safer bet.

Freddie decided that he and Roundears would walk the journey to Ballinasloe, a distance of about seventy miles, and from there they would try and stow aboard a train to Dublin, jumping train just before they got to Heuston station, the Dublin terminus from the west.

The seventy mile trek to Ballinasloe would take them at least three days. Before they set off they went on an all out hunting spree, catching as many easily portable creatures as they could. They also brought a knapsack full of berries, some sweet cake that Gert had baked and of course a healthy dose of rabbit pie. Four other foxes from the area between Ballynahinch and Clifden decided that they would embark on the trip with them, and the party set off full of high spirits.

The weather was kind to them and on the way they had some reasonably good hunting. Freddie with his experience of team hunting from the academy organised the group into small hunting parties and they actually succeeded in catching three ducks on their first night. The others were very impressed with Freddie's team skills and on the journey he began to teach them some of the techniques he had been lucky enough to learn at the academy. Of course the foxes travelled by night, extending sometimes into the early morning before human beings had emerged from their slumber. There were a number of fox resting places or travelling dens along the route which were known to one of the party and Freddie made note of them for use if he should ever be travelling that route again. There were also one or two fox boarding houses where for the price of a few duck feathers they would get a bite to eat and a safe haven, but luckily they did not have to avail of these as the weather was mild and dry and with what they managed to catch as they went along and the supplies they had brought with them they did not go hungry.

They arrived in Ballinasloe station three days before the confraternity was due to start. Ballinasloe was a good five days walk from Dublin so if they didn't succeed in getting a train they would miss a major part of the proceedings.
They holed up in a field overlooking the station and found a spot in a nearby ditch big enough to accommodate them all so that they could observe the trains coming and going. This observation point was well known to the foxes and in fact had been built by foxes for the very purpose of watching the movement of the trains. You will often find as you travel around the Irish countryside little holes and burrows that you might think have been formed accidentally. In fact you will find that a lot of them have been built by animals as observation points or travelling dens. The foxes were waiting for a night train, preferably a goods train, that would arrive in Dublin during the night or early morning.
There are two ways of stowing a ride on a train, one is the

quite dangerous one of clinging on underneath the carriage between the various chains and gantries that are to be found under railway carriages and the other is to stow away on board one of the carriages. The latter is only possible of course in a goods train and it presents an obvious difficulty; it is easy enough getting into the carriage while it is being loaded up, but getting out of the carriage at the other end could be pretty tricky. The foxes noticed a goods train being loaded up nearing completion at about seven that evening. They felt this would be the train for them, and certainly if it was leaving at around eight or nine it would get into Dublin in the dead of night, an ideal time for foxes to make their way around the big city.

After some discussion it was decided that Freddie would go and investigate but the likelihood was that they wouldn't try to board the train until the following night after having hatched a plan. Freddie went down on his own to reconnoitre the train as it was being loaded. He crept stealthily along the railway bank making sure he wasn't seen. The carriages were being loaded one by one by porters using barrows.
In between the porters' trips Freddie crept into one of the carriages to see what the accommodation was like. Frankly it was ideal; it had ventilation openings and the cargo, which consisted of bags of oats and barley, was being loaded in racks.
Freddie realised that the ventilation openings were probably for some other animals and then he remembered that the Ballinasloe horse fair was being held that week. Quite a stroke of luck really. Obviously the horses had been brought down on the train and the oats were being brought back. Freddie then came out again and looked at the security barriers to close the carriage. He thought it just might be possible if one fox stayed on the outside to open the carriage from outside before the train arrived in

Dublin thus allowing his companions to escape. He then had another look underneath the railway carriage and found one area where the floor boards were quite loose and there was an ideal cavity which would just about accommodate a medium sized fox. Freddie formulated his plan; he would stay in the cavity underneath the carriageway and as the train arrived into Dublin he would try to open the bar of the carriageway using a rope. To do this he would have to climb up to the roof of the train; It wouldn't be easy but it might just be possible.

He went back and he explained his plan to the others. They thought it was about the best one going and they felt that if they didn't succeed in opening the carriage door they would just have to make a run for it as best they could when they arrived at Dublin railway station. One of them wanted to try and go for that evening's train, but they decided they would wait until the following night to give them all an opportunity to look at the railway station so that they would know exactly what to do when the time came.

The following morning the six foxes kept a look out to see if they could spot the same train coming back again. It duly appeared only this time it was loaded with horses. They watched them being taken off and being brought to be sold in the large fair green at the other side of the town. There was no doubt they were fine looking animals and quite friendly in their own right but Freddie couldn't help wondering how many of them would be used in hunting down his fellow foxes. Ballinasloe used to have one of the biggest horse fairs in all of Europe and the Irish horses were renowned for their strength and speed. In the nineteenth century military spies used to be sent to the fair at Ballinasloe to keep an eye on which countries were buying large quantities of horses in case they were preparing for war! It was still the biggest horse fair in the country but horses now were sold mainly for hunting rather than warfare or farm work, and the fair nowadays was nothing compared to what it used to be in the old days.

That night the six foxes crept down to the railway station with Freddie in the lead. Freddie pointed out the second last carriage which he knew had the secret hiding place underneath and they waited about fifty yards away from the end of the train until it was fully loaded up. Then the porters went right to the front of the train and they began closing the doors. While this happened all the foxes darted in to the carriage and Freddie crept underneath the train and found out his little cubby hole and secured himself into it. He had to press his paws on either side to make sure he wouldn't fall out and there was no doubt he was going to have a pretty uncomfortable ride.

All of the other foxes were very impressed with Freddie's bravery and resourcefulness and they whispered encouragement to him from the railway carriage above. The foxes in the carriage had a wonderful comfortable place; there was loads of space and they even decided they would pilfer some of the oats. They weren't very tasty but it was fun to get something for nothing from humans for a change!

The previous night Freddie had found a small section of rope and formed a loop in it and this he had slung over his shoulder. When the train was about an hour out of Ballinasloe, Freddie decided to make his move. The foxes in the carriage all wished him good luck. Then with some difficulty he made his way to the gap between the end carriage and their own carriage.

This he did by creeping between the steel gantries on the underside of the carriage. It was a difficult business but he made it. At the gap between the two carriages there was a steel ladder and this Freddie was able to negotiate without any difficulty. (Foxes really do have excellent climbing ability, much more so than dogs and almost as good as cats. A vertical ladder would be cub's play to an agile fox like Freddie). Our hero then crept along the roof and loosened his rope down over the handle to the railway carriage. This was going to be tricky and he began to pull the rope out to disengage the latch. After a few minutes he succeeded and then the next thing was to pull the latch up so that the carriage could be opened. Freddie wound the rope around his shoulder and putting the rope in his mouth he pulled and pulled and pulled. However the latch was extremely heavy and stiff and he was only

Freddie's midnight adventure.

making very poor progress.
Then suddenly; **disaster!** As Freddie was heaving as hard as he could the old rope he had snapped, and not only that, Freddie went sprawling along the roof of the train and fell off at the other side!
Somewhat dazed, he picked himself up to see the last carriage disappearing into the distance. This was an absolute catastrophe! He had no idea where he was or how to get home, and he had no idea what would happen the other foxes when they got to Dublin. He certainly wouldn't make it to the confraternity but that was least of the problems on his mind at that moment!
Then Freddie saw a glimmer of hope; the train was now going around in a wide circle to avoid a river and a deep ravine below. If Freddie cut along down the ravine and swam across the river he just might be able to make it to the train at the other side after it crossed the bridge. Freddie ran his almighty best and when he got to the river he dived in and was halfway across in one bound. Foxes aren't great swimmers but Freddie would have won an Olympic gold if anyone had seen him on that occasion! He got out at the other side and could see the train approaching. He had a high hill to climb of about one hundred yards and he was almost out of breath but climb it he did. He just got to the top of the hill as the train was passing and with one leap he managed to grip on to the gantry of the last carriageway.

Roundears as you may have guessed was frantic at this stage and was sure that Freddie had been lost or had fallen under the wheels of the train. Freddie managed to creep back to the area under his own carriageway and was able to whisper up to them that he was allright, but that things were going to be tricky when they got to Dublin. Looking back on this particular adventure in later life Freddie could never understand how he was able to run so fast or how he was able to swim so quickly or make the final great leap at the end. It was a tale that he was to tell to his grandchildren and great grand children, and many of his friends who heard the tale thought he must surely have been exaggerating. But for the witness of the other foxes nobody would have believed that he could have performed such *gaisces*, as Connemara foxes call heroic deeds. However, as Freddie would often state later, desperate circumstances can bring out hidden resources and strengths in a fox that he never knew he had.

The train arrived in Dublin at about two in the morning, a time of the night when foxes are at their best and humans tend to be somewhat drowsy. Freddie jumped down and crept up to the edge of platform number four at Heuston Station. The platform was dimly lit and he was able to hide out under a bench on the platform while the porters began unloading. He knew he would have to act quickly if there was to be any chance of saving his comrades from capture or worse.

As the time came to open the door of the fox's carriageway, Freddie got ready for action. Luckily only one porter was opening the doors, and when he had the first door open Freddie made a quick dart and nipped him on the right heel. The porter was so taken aback that he turned around and almost toppled over in amazement "What's that?" he cried out. At this Freddie barked "Quick lads run for it" and out his five comrades scurried. "What's going on" shouted the porter, "there are some wolves or something inside in the carriage". His friend came running down with a lamp and what looked to Freddie like a shotgun but by this time the foxes were half way down the track.
"What's wrong Jack?" asked the porter's comrade.
"I'm not sure, I'm not sure" Jack replied uncertainly and still a bit dazed. "They were either wolves or very large

cats , I couldn't see in the dim light".
"You've been having a bit too much of the hard stuff" replied Jack's companion. "We haven't had wolves in Ireland for two hundred years. Come on, let's get this stuff unloaded and don't let me hear any more talk about wolves at this hour of night".
The foxes had made their escape all right but the next difficulty was finding their destination, and while Roundears was particularly proud of Freddie's gallant actions she decided she had better leave her congratulations until they had actually reached safety. The group had arranged to stay with an aunt of Roundears, whose burrow was quite close to Clonoulty, and Roundears had pretty good directions.
However Roundears' aunt,, who name was Jingo, lived about three miles away and by the time the foxes were getting close to her den it was getting bright and motor cars were beginning to come out in their droves, even at that early hour of the morning. Freddie had never seen so many cars and some of the other foxes were looking around in amazement at the strange sights of Dublin. "Come on lads." said Freddie "We can do our sight seeing later, let's find our hideout and fast".
Dogs and motor cars are the two main enemies of foxes in the city and the foxes met more than their fair share of both on that early morning. They had to redouble their steps on more than one occasion. They were lucky that there were six of them and because of their numbers they were able to frighten off one terrier who looked all set for a fight.
They eventually made their destination in the early morning light. Jingo had been waiting up for them for the past three nights and was looking about anxiously. She was delighted when she finally saw them and had a hearty welcome for all. She had a meal all ready in her neat and well laid out burrow, and the exhausted foxes set to with gusto. Everybody had wonderful tales about

Freddie's gallantry and while their spirits were high nevertheless they were so tired that they were all sound asleep within an hour of their arrival.

The following evening was the date before the confraternity was due to start and the foxes had a night free for sightseeing. It was a tricky business sightseeing around Dublin because even late at night and into the early morning the enemies of the fox were out and about. Nevertheless, the foxes like six gay Lotharios ventured out and took their chances.

They couldn't get over the strange way that people in Dublin lived with all the houses so close together. Most of them disliked the busy hum of the traffic and found it very difficult to get used to. They were amazed however at the amount of free food that was to be found in the city late at night in bins outside shops and restaurants in particular. They couldn't quite figure out how all the human beings gathered so densely together in one place could live together and they couldn't figure out where they got their food from. Another thing they noticed was the way in which the city never seemed to go to sleep. In the countryside things seemed to have a natural order of wakening and then going to sleep but the city always seemed to be awake, always prowling around and always presenting hidden dangers.

Some of the foxes were quite taken with the idea of city life, its excitement and the plentiful food that seemed to be available, but Freddie and Roundears knew instinctively that Connemara was the place for them and despite the fact that there definitely seemed to be some easy pickings in Dublin, they knew that life in the city couldn't compare to the free, wild life of the mountains and the moors.

When they got back in the early morning they all sat down together in Jingo's burrow and began to talk. First

they spoke about relatives and friends that they knew. Freddie enquired after his cousins Alexis and Sylvester. "Well" Jingo replied "Alexis I will have you know is doing very well, this year she is mating with a fox over in Foxrock, whose territory includes the dustbins of two politicians and one pop star if you don't mind. Why the last time I met Alexis she told me half jokingly that she wouldn't at all mind becoming a pet fox".
Freddie was pleased in one sense to hear that Alexis was doing so well but he thought it rather a pity that she had become so urbanised. He couldn't get over his rural prejudice that living out of dustbins, no matter how wealthy the owners of those dustbins, was really no life for a fox.
"And what about Sylvester?" Freddie asked.
Jingo thought for a moment and then Freddie could see a strange look coming into her eye.
"Why, ehm, yes, Sylvester is doing very well too, very well indeed. At the moment he's got himself a very prominent position. But look Freddie, You're nearly out of Berry juice. I'll get you some more."
And Jingo hurried off to pour out some Haw-Berry juice for her guests.

The talk inevitably then turned to the confraternity which was about to start on the following evening. The foxes argued among themselves about what Clarion was up to and what changes he would propose making. These are certainly exciting times to be a fox thought Freddie as he watched the sun coming up.
All the foxes fell silent as the sun appeared over the horizon, each with his own thoughts about the great events that would unfold at the ancient burrow of Clonoulty that following evening. Soon the preparations they had made and the long and dangerous journey they had undertaken would come to its culmination. Each fox felt as if he had a date with destiny, and they looked

forward to the following night with a mixture of excitement, trepidation and wonder.

Freddie was quite tired as he put his head down to sleep. All would be revealed the following evening he said to himself in that phlegmatic way of his. And so it was.

CHAPTER 7

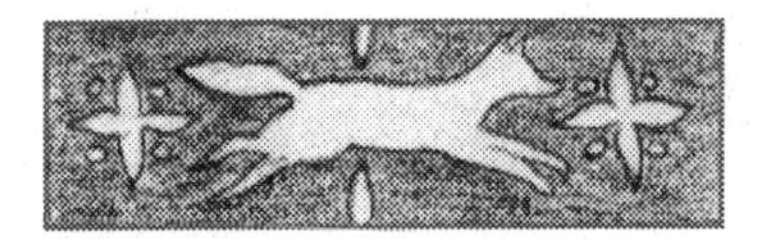

THE GREAT FOX CONFRATERNITY OF CLONOULTY

Ireland being one of the few countries in Europe where the Fox is still reasonably successful as a species, the confraternity had, as you can imagine, aroused considerable interest internationally.
You will know of course that foxes have various means of sending information to their colleagues and friends abroad. The most usual and dependable means of sending international messages from an island like Ireland is that of putting certain scratchings on cargo boxes, which are used in transport ships to foreign countries. In each country foxes are detailed especially to keep a look out around ports for any signs or messages from other countries of important goings on. By these means Clarion had made sure that news of the Clonoulty confraternity was well flagged in other countries, and it was rumoured that some of the fox leaders were going to come from abroad.
Usually when a famous fox came from abroad he travelled with a small retinue, normally stowing away in the hold of a ship. More recently, famous foxes had started making foreign journeys by hiding in the luggage holds of aeroplanes, though as you can imagine this required a good deal of planning and organisation.

On the night when the confraternity was to start, at about one o'clock in the morning, anyone travelling through, or walking in the Phoenix Park would have seen an extraordinary sight; literally hundreds, if not thousands of foxes were converging on the park from all parts of Dublin and indeed all parts of Ireland. They were making for a well known (to foxes that is) Oak tree with a small opening at the base into which each one disappeared as he arrived. There were so many foxes that before long there was a huge congregation of them all disappearing one by one into the entrance. Several people saw the huge collection of foxes and newspaper reports were to appear over the next few days about the strange goings on that were seen and heard around the Phoenix Park that night, with all sorts of far flung theories about what was happening, none of them of course being anywhere near to guessing that a fox confraternity was afoot.

Many nature spotters over the next few days came to see if they could figure out what was going on and some collected around the Oak tree. However like all burrows Clonoulty had more than one entrance and more than one exit. Clonoulty is in fact one of the biggest burrows in Europe. It is rumoured to have over forty two different entrances and exits and a room or compartment for every day of the year.

On entering the base of the Oak tree Freddie, Roundears and his companions went down a long winding passageway to about twenty feet below ground. Then they emerged into a large entrance hall where they were met by two receptionist foxes who asked them what their main interest was and indicated where they were supposed to go.

The whole confraternity was really very well organised and supplies were laid on so that foxes could stay down in the burrow for several days at a time without having to emerge. This way human suspicions weren't aroused too much by the goings on below ground.

Clonoulty in olden days was the primary seat of ancient Irish fox learning. It was here that the code of honour was first put together and here that the rules of fox behaviour governing territories and rules of demarcation were decided upon in the third century. Of course there aren't nearly as many foxes working there now as used to in those far off days but it is still a very impressive burrow, and if you ever get a chance (though this is unlikely), you should visit it. Its principal feature is a huge assembly hall, the roof of which is a type of opalescent rock which allows light through from a shallow lake overhead. Foxes, I have already explained, don't depend on their eyes as much as we do and even some quite small quantities of light penetrating into a burrow is more than enough for them.

In all, there were almost two thousand foxes gathered in the assembly hall for the confraternity. These were arranged in great semi-circular tiers ascending up to a height of twenty foxes. Freddie was about in the fifteenth row back but nevertheless because of the semi-circular arrangement he had an excellent view of the goings on and could hear every word that was spoken. Some of the foxes involved in the ceremony were decked out in tremendous ceremonial splendour. Freddie spied in the distance his former school teacher Slimlegs Whitepatch, who had on a long white robe similar to the one he had worn in graduation only a different colour. Obviously Slimlegs had some particular role to perform, probably something to do with education, thought Freddie.

The entire hall was a buzz of excitement and then a long lonesome whistling howl was heard from the side entrance to the hall and all the foxes fell silent. An announcement was made by an enormously fat chaxer with a great booming voice and a commanding manner; "All foxes pray be upstanding for the arrival of the leader of all the foxes, winner of two all Ireland lamping championships, Commander of the Ancient Order of the

Furry Paw, Leader and Convenor of this historic confraternity, the benign, the merciful, the wise Clarion, the wily fox of Inchicore!"
Clarion entered preceded by two young standard bearers

Foxes, though you might not think it to look at them, are very fond of a bit of a show, and love nothing better than a procession with standard bearers and music.

each carrying a holly bush and followed by a retinue of sixteen foxes in pairs, each wearing a splendidly coloured gown. Then followed the contingent of fox leaders from abroad, each carrying a plant or other symbol from his native land. Clarion himself was simply dressed apart

from the two golden tips that he wore at the ends of his ears, which were a sign of his leadership. He was quite an old fox but he still had the well known twinkle in his eye. He could not be described as having a majestic bearing, but he had a very appealing though none the less shrewd demeanour which caused him to instantly win favour and respect among all those present. He walked quite briskly for a fox of his years to the centre of the stage, where he was joined by the other important foxes and the representatives from abroad.
Clarion went to the rostrum and coughed to clear his throat for the beginning of his speech as the hall fell silent.

"My fellow foxes" he began in his mellifluous voice "these are strange and difficult times for the fox. We are under pressure from our old enemies the human beings as never before. Many of our number under the pressure of these attacks have begun to disobey the rules which for centuries have kept the fox species alive and prosperous. The style of living of many of our members is now changing. In rural areas foxes are driven to the more and more lonely and secluded places and the ancient rituals of fox brotherhood and fox solidarity are beginning to collapse. At the same time many foxes have come to live in the great cities and have adopted a lifestyle very different to that of their ancestors. We do not know what the result of all these great changes will be, but we do know that there are times when it may be appropriate to adjust codes of honour and codes of behaviour to meet changing circumstances."
"For this reason I have asked so many foxes to come to this confraternity from all parts of Ireland and some from abroad in order that we may review each aspect of the code of honour to determine whether we need new rules of behaviour and whether perhaps some of the old rules may be disbanded."

"This confraternity will have groups which will be led by a distinguished member of Foxdom to look into each aspect of the code of honour. Every two days we will have reports back to a meeting here in this great hall which will be presided over by myself. Every other day we will have an address from one of our distinguished foreign visitors. Let us hope that our work together will not only enable the fox species to survive but will also enable each fox to lead a better and happier life and enable him to contribute to the welfare of foxes in his local community and to the welfare of all of Foxdom."
"We must all remember my dear fellow foxes" Clarion went on in that charming humble way of his that made him so well loved, "that in the course of our deliberations here we will not only be dealing with matters of practical concern, we will also have to ask ourselves many deep and often difficult questions. What is the purpose of our time here on this earth as foxes? How can we help the fox species to grow and develop? These are questions that perhaps we do not often reflect on, but I hope and I pray that all foxes who have taken the trouble to come to this great gathering will give of their best efforts and their deepest consideration to planning out a strategy for the future of the Fox."
"I believe" he concluded "that this confraternity of Clonoulty will go down in history as one of the most important events in the history of the Fox in Ireland!"

A great howl went up from the mighty assembly of foxes when this speech was finished and anyone passing by twenty feet overhead in the Phoenix Park would have heard a strange humming noise which caused the entire ground to vibrate slightly.

After Clarion's speech had ended the foxes all divided up in groups and went off into various compartments to commence their deliberations. Clonoulty is an extremely complex series of warrens and burrows at varying different levels and it is very easy for even a fox to lose his way. You can easily go down a long tunnel into a chamber and continue going and then emerge at a high level balcony over the first large chamber from which you had started. Most of the chambers however eventually make their way back into the great central hall underneath the lake, so as long as you know where to go from there you won't go too badly astray.

The various discussions which took place at Clonoulty were very complicated, and it would not be possible to explain them in detail in this short book. There were discussions on such things as foxes helping each other, team hunting etiquette and procedures (always tricky), how to settle territorial disputes, whether or not some of the more old fashioned rules should be abandoned, the whole process of education of foxes, whether the prohibition on killing entire families of prey should be deleted and many other complex and weighty matters. Freddie, despite all his interest in philosophy found the sessions pretty tough going and he would often finish the night's discussion with a roaring headache. He stayed the first four days down in the burrow before emerging for a days break and he and Roundears were so absorbed with the thoughts of the confraternity that they almost lost their way home to Jingo's burrow.

Among the most enjoyable aspects of the confraternity were the speeches from the great fox leaders. Clarion himself gave a talk on the importance of team work for foxes. This was very much to Freddie's liking as he had a particular interest in team hunting. However Clarion was making the point that teamwork was not only useful for hunting but that foxes as a group being under such pressure would find it pretty difficult to progress at any level unless they helped one another out.

One of the visitor foxes whom Freddie also found very interesting was a fox called Mintion. He was a small shy Cyprus fox who had travelled by boat all the way from his native island. Cyprus foxes are extremely shy, and everyone could see that it was difficult for Mintion to make speeches and chair meetings. He was the kind of fox who, if he ever came across humans, would immediately dash away and look for somewhere to hide, engaging in a rapid digging action as a type of nervous reaction. Nevertheless those who got to know Mintion soon found him to be a great and loyal friend and also a very deep thinker. He had a very saintly smile and true to his Cyprus fox nature he urged caution in changing any of the major rules of the code of honour. While he accepted the importance of reforming some of the rules, he thought that it was very important not to throw out the good with the bad and he felt that there was no need for a root and branch reform.

Mintion, though a very deep thinker, was an extremely shy Cyprus fox, with delicate features and shy, sensitive eyes.

One of the star performers of the confraternity was a youngish fox by the name of Thomas Jefferson Yowla. He was an Arctic fox with a beautiful white coat such as most of the other foxes had never seen before. He also had stunning pale blue eyes and many of the Irish foxes queued up just to get a look at him. Thomas Jefferson, or T.J. as he was known to his friends, had a very go-ahead style. Apparently he had arrived in Ireland by helicopter no less, having stowed away with his retinue in an army helicopter that was doing exercises from Finland where he lived.

This show of bravado was a cause of great admiration among the local foxes. Yowla had a great ringing voice and a marvellous stage presence and all the foxes who came to listen to him were riveted by his speeches. However they soon found out that there was more than just style to T.J.Yowla. While he was all for reforms and in particular for trying to get the younger foxes and the urban foxes back into the honour system, nevertheless it was clear that he fully believed that the code of honour should be upheld. In fact he felt there was no future for the fox, either urban or rural, without it.

Thomas Jefferson Yowla, with his ready smile and ringing voice was a great hit at Clonoulty.

A fox who took a somewhat different view was a fox by the name of Gun Shank, who had travelled by ferry boat from Germany. He was of the belief that rules should be made entirely voluntary and that it should really be up to each fox to make up his own mind how he lived his life. Certainly it would be useful for a fox to help another fox but there shouldn't be any rules and regulations about it, he said.

He was certainly a very persuasive speaker and many of the foxes felt there was a great deal of sense in what he said. Before long it began to emerge that there was something of Yowla wing and a Gun Shank wing emerging. This was the last thing that Clarion wanted because he was very anxious to make sure that whatever happened there was agreement among the foxes and that there wouldn't be two separate groups going off doing different things.

The education of foxes was one important matter which received wide debate, and in particular the whole issue of "the message of fear" as Slimlegs used to call it at school. There was no doubt that a lot of foxes had been brought up in fear of the terrible consequences that would happen if they didn't obey the code of honour and the Gun Shank wing in particular was anxious to have the message of fear replaced with the message of hope, that is that wonderful things would happen to a fox if he did do the right things. Yowla and his group agreed to this for the most part but they still claimed that there was room for an occasional dose of fear as well. The foxes soon learned that despite his charming ways Yowla had a look in his eye that could cow any fox into silence, including even Gun Shank on one occasion (but then perhaps it was the pale blue eyes that did it).

One of the things that was in need of reform, and most sides agreed on this, was the large number of niggling little rules that were in the code of honour such as not eating certain types of food at certain times of the year,

for example no rabbit stew during the month of August. It was agreed by fairly universal consent to drop a lot of these rules and this didn't cause too much trouble with anybody apart from one crusty old fox called Lucius Eliot Cramblefever, an elderly chaxer from France who didn't seem to be able to get on with anyone, not even the accommodating and reasonable Mintion.
"It looks as if our respected chaxer L.E.Cramblefever will have to set up his own confraternity", Clarion would say resignedly but still with the mischievous twinkle in his eye.

There were also some small regulations that Freddie wasn't too anxious to see going. A lot of the local fox groups had their own regulations and one that he was very attached to was the one that affected all the foxes around Connaught, namely that the immediate grounds of Ballynahinch castle should be respected and protected from fox attack.
Freddie was directly involved in the group that was discussing this issue and things certainly weren't going his way. He was one of the very few foxes who wanted to retain this rule even though he himself wasn't altogether sure why. Freddie found unfortunately, that he wasn't a very good debater, and important points would often occur to him after his turn for speaking had passed.
The debate on this issue was held in a fairly large warren with about twenty foxes participating. Things were going badly with only four other foxes being in favour of retaining the rule and the final vote about to be taken when who should walk in but Clarion himself!
All the foxes stood up as a mark of respect and he asked to know what was being discussed. When he was told that they were just about to change the rule concerning the respect due to the grounds of Ballynahinch Castle, Clarion paused and looked into the air and smiled enigmatically.

"I think it would be a great pity" he said gravely after a long and meaningful pause "if the respect due to the former home of the great Humbledrum Dick were to be discontinued" and he smiled his charming open smile and looked at all the foxes present.
Well that was it really. There was no arguing against that kind of simple statement and even those foxes who were in favour of dropping the special standing of Ballynahinch began to change their minds. Clarion got up and left and shortly afterwards it was agreed that Balynahinch would continue to have a special place among the foxes of Connemara, of West Connaught and of North Clare. Freddie and Roundears were delighted with this turn of events even though it did in effect mean that part of their own natural territory, which included one edge of Ballynahinch Castle grounds, would continue to be out of bounds for them. Still it was worth making sacrifices for "old decency" as foxes used to call these things. This intervention of Clarion's certainly taught Freddie a lesson on how to influence your fellow fox!

When all the weighty issues had been entirely debated the various groups began to report back to Clarion and his teams who busily began to draw up revised sets of regulations and sets of proposals for approval. On the final day of the confraternity Clarion announced the main findings of the various groups. These were all duly voted on and agreed. Where agreement couldn't be reached Clarion had the deciding vote.

The main decisions that were made by the confraternity were to reform the educational system of foxes, to get rid of a lot of the minor rules of the code of honour, to make some of the regulations of the code of honour subject to local fox councils which were to be established, to place an increased emphasis on foxes engaging in team work including, much to Freddie's delight, team hunting, to place less emphasis on fear in bringing up young foxes and to teach young foxes to be more confident and hopeful.

The main provisions of the code of honour however were upheld. Foxes were still to be bound by the code and it was agreed that foxes that regularly broke the code were to be cast out from their group and were to be ignored by all other foxes.

Many in the Gun Shank wing were not at all happy with this but nevertheless the majority of foxes thought that the whole thrust of the confraternity had been very good and had made excellent progress. The whole thing was hugely optimistic really and all of the foxes who were at the confraternity from all the four corners of Ireland went back to their homes fully refreshed and with bright thoughts for the future.

If you ever ask a fox who attended the confraternity what they remember most, they will almost all mention the speech from Clarion which closed the proceedings on the last night. This was something that Freddie remembered to the last days of his life.

"My dear fellow foxes" Clarion had begun, "you have all come here over the past long weeks", (remember a week is a long time for a fox) " and you have spent your time deliberating and turning over various things in your minds to determine what will be the future of Foxdom. We have made many weighty decisions here and we believe in our own way that these are decisions of great importance."

"We must always remember however our own role in the great scheme of things. Many of the decisions we have made may not be absolutely the right ones, though they are the best decisions we could make. We should remember that many of the great foxes that have gone before us, some of them here in this very chamber, have also made great and weighty decisions, sometimes they

were right and sometimes they were not. Whatever we do as foxes we should remember that there is a goodness in nature. Those of us foxes lucky enough to live close to nature in the countryside will probably know what I mean, but even those foxes who live in the city can often see the goodness and the peace that lives in nature and the natural order of things. Remember this above all else my dear fellow foxes; Always trust in providence. Always trust in goodness. There are times when you may even trust in human beings. For after a long life I have come to one conclusion, that a fox who believes in goodness will achieve goodness and will experience goodness."
When Clarion had finished the entire hall remained absolutely silent (you try gathering two thousand foxes in a room and get them to remain absolutely silent). They didn't quite know what Clarion meant but they could all see that he meant something and that whatever he meant he was probably right. Clarion just had that sort of way about him, and all the foxes present felt that they were very lucky to have been in the presence of a great leader like him.

I needn't tell you that the various goings on over the previous two weeks in the middle of Dublin's Phoenix Park had, despite the best efforts of the confraternity organisers, raised some interest among the human community. The various comings and goings had not gone unobserved and gangs of nature watchers began to come to the Phoenix Park to see if they could spot the foxes and figure out what they were up to. Some of the organisers had become quite worried in case their great secret would be found out and the famous burrow of Clonoulty would be discovered. They decided therefore that for two years thereafter no further ceremonies of any kind would be held at Clonoulty. Furthermore they decided that on this last night it would be necessary to spread confusion among their human observers. For that reason once the ceremonies were over and Clarion had made his formal farewell to the foxes they were all divided up into equal numbers and positioned around the forty two different exits from Clonoulty burrow, some of them as much as a mile distant from the main entrance underneath the ancient oak tree. At a predetermined time, about half past four in the morning, a set of fox whistles (inaudible to human ears) were set off and suddenly from every one of the forty two exits, foxes began to pour out and began disappearing in all directions throughout the city of Dublin and beyond.

Those few nature watchers who were left at that hour of the morning and who hadn't seen very much happening over the previous few days, were thrown into total confusion. Foxes seemed to be literally everywhere, coming from all directions and going in all directions and the humans were out with their cameras and their tape recorders and their measuring instruments but they couldn't figure out what was going on. After about an hour of this excitement and after several of the humans had bumped into one another and started fighting one another, the way humans will, that part of Phoenix Park was nearly empty of foxes.

Freddie, Roundears and their group had decided that they would take the same route back as they had come. They had been told by the Confraternity organisers that there was a train leaving for Ballinasloe that morning at half past five so they knew they would have to hurry if they were going to make it.

As they were passing along near Parkgate street on their way to the station Freddie noticed something out of the corner of his eye that made him stop dead in his tracks. It was in the middle of a window in a bright, gaily painted building. Freddie blinked his eyes a few times to make sure he wasn't seeing things. He wasn't, for there in the middle of the window, plain for all to see was his cousin

Sylvester, with a peculiar snarling expression on his face and his paw raised in mid air as if he was just about to jump at something. Freddie looked around to see what Sylvester could have been about to leap upon and could see nothing. Even though he was in a bit of a hurry and even though he had never been that fond of Sylvester, Freddie thought that it would only be polite to go over and have a word with him.

As Freddie scurried over Sylvester made no move whatever and Freddie thought that his life in the city must have made him very careless not to be able to see that another animal was coming up to him. However as Freddie got closer he began to suspect that there was something wrong with Sylvester though he couldn't quite put his paw on what it was.

"Sylvester, Sylvester" Freddie called and he tapped on the window a few times to try to attract his attention. Then with a shock the truth dawned on him. This was Sylvester all right, but ***dead and stuffed and mounted in a glass case*** for humans to come and gape at!

Freddie was appalled at what he saw and he nearly felt dizzy when he realised what had become of his cousin. He remembered Jingo's description that he had "achieved a prominent position" and he smiled weakly at this ironic and black humour, a type of dark humour some foxes are very fond of.

Roundears had come back to see what was keeping Freddie.

"It's nothing" he lied, "just something strange in that window".. Freddie shook his head sadly. After all the wonderful things he had seen and heard at the confraternity this certainly brought him back down to earth with a jolt. He wondered what kinds of beings these humans were. He wondered how they would feel if gangs of foxes were to go around capturing human children and stuffing them and displaying them in their

dens so that their fox friends could come and have a good laugh.
"Poor old Sylvester" he thought.

Freddie didn't allow this sad event to annoy him too much and soon he was back in the high spirits of the rest of his companions. They got back as far as Ballinasloe on the train without too much incident, and on the way home to Connemara they engaged in several team hunting trips. They couldn't wait to get home to all their neighbours to tell them about the great events that had taken place.

When they got home after their long journey, the cubs were nearly fully grown and almost ready to disperse. It was decided that Foxglove would stay with them for another year but that the others would go their separate ways.
Freddie expected when he got back home that everybody would be brimming with enquiries about what had happened at the great confraternity. Indeed many foxes were full of questions, but a funny thing that you will often notice is that when you have had your nose stuck in something for a long time, you may make the mistake of thinking that everybody else is as interested in it as you are. Freddie was somewhat surprised when he got home to find that many of the foxes had continued their lives with only a passing interest at best in Clonoulty and its goings on. He was a bit disappointed in this but he was beginning to get the wisdom that comes to foxes with age, and he realised that it was part of fox nature and indeed an essential part of fox nature to be concerned with practical things. Nevertheless he did his bit to spread the new message of hope that had come from Clonoulty.

One of the suggestions that came from the confraternity was that foxes who had been at to Clonoulty were to organise meetings where they could let their fellow foxes know of the great changes that had taken place. Freddie did his best to set up these meetings but found that really they weren't very well attended. It seemed to be the same old foxes who were coming all the time. Gert and a few of her friends were very interested indeed in Clonoulty and they would ask Freddie questions late into the night about what had happened each day and what famous fox leader or chaxer had said what, and to explain in detail about the great debates and counter debates that had taken place. It was just as well Freddie had such a good memory. Some of the younger foxes of his own age had an interest too and Freddie felt that these foxes were the real hope for the future.

That winter after the confraternity was a pretty cold, wet and miserable winter around Connemara. The cubs stayed with Freddie and Roundears until December, and in fact Freddie and Roundears decided to stay together for another year. They had enjoyed each other's company very much over the previous twelve months and without speaking much about it they just decided to stay together for another season.

This winter was the first really hard winter they had ever experienced. Freddie saw many sad things; young foxes dying of the cold, an entire badger family flooded out of their set and with no-where to stay, families of Robin redbreasts with little or nothing to eat throughout the whole Winter. He was aware while all this was going on that some foxes began to raid the grounds of Ballynahinch. Freddie found this very sad but he understood it. After all it was a particularly bad winter and you couldn't expect high standards of behaviour from foxes all the time, particularly foxes whose families were starving.

Despite all the deprivations of that winter, Freddie made an effort, if he had any bit of surplus, to bring it to an older fox who might have been in trouble, starting with

his mother Gert and other relatives of his. He felt that while he was still young and strong he had a certain obligation to do this and he would also call in for a chat and talk about the things he had seen in Dublin and what had happened at the confraternity. He enjoyed doing this even though some of the foxes of his own age told him he would be better off looking after himself first, but even when they said this they knew that Freddie really was a very decent sort of fox. They had known this about him even when he was at school, how he always had a kind word for another fox who might be in trouble and they felt that was really just Freddie's way.
Food was definitely getting harder to find, not just because of the hard winter but because a lot of the farmers in Connemara were using a new type of fencing and it was becoming very difficult for foxes to raid farmyards. There was new strains of poison being put down and fewer people were keeping chickens. Freddie often in fact had somewhat anxious thoughts about the future, not so much for himself because he was by nature an optimistic fox but for the whole family of Foxdom. He wished that more foxes had gone to Clonoulty or at least had listened more to its message.

Despite the hard weather Freddie and Roundears didn't have too much difficulty surviving and they were both looking forward to the Spring when there would be a new beginning, warmer weather , leaves on the trees, and, most importantly, their second family.

Freddie was to see many happy Springs and some sad winters over the next few years. He was destined to have an eventful and exciting life. For the moment however we will leave our tale of Freddie and Roundears and their friends and enemies and return to a very different world, a world with which you may be more familiar.

CHAPTER 8

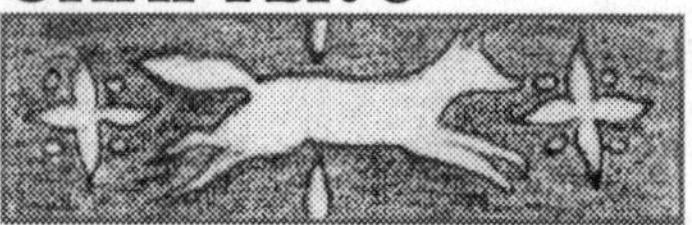

BALLYNAHINCH CASTLE

Our story now moves away from the burrows and the moors and the wild, secret and well organised world of the fox and back to the land of the human being. You may find this a bit of a pity in view of the fact that you have to live most of your life in the land of the human, except for those times when you can dream and pretend to be something else like a fox or a lion, so I won't detain you too long in the world that you are already well used to. It is however necessary to tell you a little bit about a place that you have already come across in our story, namely Ballynahinch Castle.

The grounds of Ballynahinch Castle are among the loveliest of any of the old houses of Ireland. The castle itself is almost 700 years old in parts, and was once the home of the famous pirate queen, Grace O'Malley and of the notorious O'Flaherty family, a family so fearsome that in the olden times the councillors of Galway City used to pray at every meeting for "protection from the wild O'Flahertys".

The reason however that the fox species always held the ancient castle and its grounds in high regard was because of its connection with the Martin family, in particular Richard "Trigger" Martin who lived there from 1813 to 1834.

The Martins were one of the ancient tribes of Galway, and true to the family tradition, Richard Martin was a colourful character. Richard got his nick-name, "Trigger Martin", from the fact that he was one of the most notorious duellists in Ireland, fighting many of his duels around Galway City. One of his most famous duels was fought with the deadly "Fighting Fitzgerald" who was later found to have been wearing a suit of armour under his clothes as protection, and who forever lost his reputation as a duellist after this show of cowardice! The favourite method of duelling at that time was of course the duelling pistol and Trigger Martin, or Hair Trigger Dick, being an extremely good shot, killed many an opponent with a single bullet. This ruthless and hard aspect to his personality caused him to be feared and respected throughout Ireland and Britain which were at that time joined together.

However, Trigger Martin also had a very different side to his personality. In an age when cruelty to animals was commonplace, an accepted thing you might say, Dick Martin was renowned for his kindliness to all animals. He would not tolerate anybody being cruel to an ox or horse or dog, and if, on any of his vast estates, which stretched all the way out from Galway City to Ballynahinch, any one was found mistreating an animal in his charge, then that person would be imprisoned on a small jail on the island in the middle of Ballynahinch lake, which is to be seen to this day.
This special kindliness to animals rubbed off on many of the people around Connemara, especially those close to Ballynahinch, who began to develop a special relationship with animals of all kinds.

Dick Martin was a member of Parliament in London while he lived at Ballynahinch, and one of the things he is best remembered for is the campaign he waged in England to improve the conditions of animals. In fact he was responsible for the Prevention of Cruelty to Animals Act, and he was a co-founder of the Royal Society for Prevention of Cruelty to Animals (R.S.P.C.A.). Similar societies were later established all over the world. For these many acts of kindness to animals Dick Martin was given another nickname, that of "Humanity Dick". Perhaps the word "humanity" doesn't have the same meaning for foxes as it does for us, and that may explain why the name became changed in Fox lore to "Humbledrum Dick".

The portrait of Humanity Dick Martin

In any event, knowledge of, and respect for Humanity Dick's great actions soon spread among the foxes of Ireland and that is why Ballynahinch Castle was given a special dispensation to be free from fox attacks, something that has lasted almost down to the present day.

If you ever manage to visit Ballynahinch Castle and you go into the entrance hall you will see over the fireplace a striking portrait of Humanity Dick. In it you will see the hard tough face of a West Galway man, but in the eyes you can undoubtedly make out the twinkle of human kindness which you will often find in even the toughest of men. Humanity became known as the King of Connemara, and perhaps it was his kindness more than his ruthlessness that earned him the special title of King.

Another famous owner of Ballynahinch Castle was Prince Rangit Singh, the famous Indian cricketer. Rangi, as he was known, was a fabulously wealthy prince, the Maharaja of Nawanagar in fact, and he owned Ballynahinch for ten years around the 1920's. He used to come to the castle every year from India and stay for up to six months. He had his own railway carriage and used to come out from Galway at the time when there still were trains to small towns in Ireland. A lot of the foxes around Ballynahinch were delighted to see this because it meant that they could get free rides in and out to see the sights of Galway. Whenever news came of Rangi coming, Freddie's ancestors used to play around the tracks waiting for the great, opulent train carriage to arrive and for the fabulously dressed Maharaja to descend. The local people of Ballynahinch used to light firecrackers along the rail tracks before Rangi used to arrive and the foxes used to stay up all day just to watch these being set off. What they enjoyed even more was the sight of Rangi descending from the train with his entourage and he dressed in the most beautiful clothes you ever saw. Silver and gold flowing robes and head dress like a peacock! And the motor cars he used to have! Neither the foxes nor the people around Connemara had ever seen anything the like of them before.

Foxes, as I may have told you, are very fond of a show, and tales of Rangi were told among the foxes of Connemara for many generations after he had stopped coming to Ballynahinch.

Prince Rangit Singh

Ballynahinch Castle is now a hotel, one of finest in all of Ireland. It has wonderful grounds and lakes and fisheries and it is full of the true tradition of Connemara hospitality.

The maintenance of the hotel, at the time of Freddie, fell to an efficient young man by the name of Mr. Herbert Bannon. Mr. Bannon was very proud of the hotel in which he worked and did his very best to ensure that everything was ship shape and right for his guests. He was a thin, active man with a pleasant smile and gold rimmed glasses that glinted in the moonlight.

While Mr. Bannon was primarily engaged in working indoors at the hotel, he also took a great interest in the grounds of the great castle. He enjoyed watching the many little birds and squirrels that found their homes in the trees around the castle and in general he found, as many people do, that the grounds of Ballynahinch have a special magic all of their own.

There was one thing however that he was finding a bit of a nuisance over the past two years, something which he had never noticed before. Foxes! They had, for the first time that he could remember, started raiding around the grounds, rooting around in the rubbish, leaving things in a bit of a mess and generally making a perfect nuisance of themselves.

Mr. Bannon paced thoughtfully over the beautifully polished clay floor tiles in the main entrance hall of Ballynahinch. He picked up a piece of antique silverware and examined it. He would have to take steps to deal with these foxes he decided as he walked back into the dining room with its magnificent ornate fireplace. He would take steps that would get rid of them once and for all.

He looked out at the Owenmore River and soon forgot about foxes as he was carried away by the river's magic as it flowed off down towards Derryclare, down past the old railway bridge where Rangi used to arrive, down past the deep fishing pool, down in fact to a place not too far from a burrow where a fox called Freddie lived.

And with the river's flow we will leave the human, and return for a time to the vulpine world, where, unknown to themselves, the foxes appear to have made a new enemy in the person of Mr. Herbert Bannon, as if foxes didn't have enough enemies already.

For I hear that among our friends the foxes, apart altogether from any new enemies they may have, things are not going as well as they might for a variety of other reasons.

CHAPTER 9

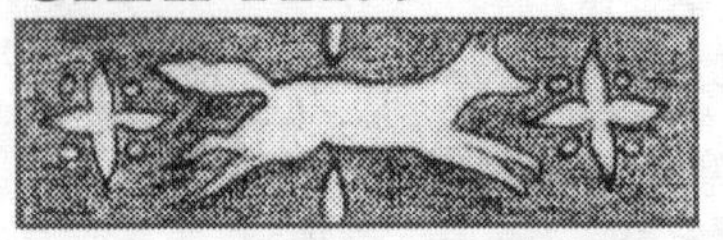

A HARD WINTER.

As we leave the world of the human let us also move our story forward a few years and see what has become of our vulpine heroes in that time.

On our return to the animal kingdom we find that Freddie is now seven years old. Many things have happened to him in the last number of years, and many changes have come into the vulpine world in that, for foxes, lengthy period of time.

Incidentally, if you think it's rather hard on foxes not living terribly long and being considered quite elderly by the time you or I would still be considered spring chickens, then don't think that at all. For a fox, the seven or eight years he normally lives is just as long as the seventy we may have (if we're lucky), and if you told an eight year old fox who had lived a hard life in the wild that he had another sixty or so years to live he would probably look at you aghast.
Most foxes, like most living creatures, have a good idea when they have been around for long enough and wouldn't like to extend their time too much. (Of course if you asked them, they might like another year or two, but then wouldn't we all!).
In any event foxes manage to cram as much living into their few years in this world as we do into ours, many of them more so, so you needn't feel too sorry for them because their lives are short by our standards; They probably feel somewhat sorry for us living so long!
Freddie over the past six years has seen a lot of changes

and many happy and many sad things have happened to him. He is now a very different fox from the fox we have met earlier on in our pages. He is still cheerful and helpful to other foxes but he has developed a certain wisdom and a slightly melancholy and sad look in his eye. He is now a more dignified fox, and like most foxes who have lived to his age he has developed an extraordinary cunning and ability to survive in difficult circumstances. Unlike many foxes of his age however he has developed a tendency to reflect over the great fox events that he has witnessed in his lifetime.

On the particular fine October morning of our return to the vulpine world, Freddie was half way up the mountain of Ben Lettery, after a useful morning's grouse hunting, looking down over Derryclare lake and thinking over the main events of his life.

He thought first of the many cubs to whom he had been a father and provider, particularly his first batch and his favourites, Ratcatcher and Foxglove. He had lost contact with them now of course, but he would instantly recognise any of his cubs if he came across one of them in the wild. Perhaps it was just as well that foxes lose contact with their cubs after a year or two he thought. So many of them were likely to come to an unpleasant end these days that it was better not to dwell on keeping in touch.

He thought of how some of his cubs were shrewd and how others were less so, how some had pleasant helpful personalities and others seemed to be only concerned with themselves. He had taken special care with these last types to try to ensure that they understood the code of honour and for the most part he could say that any cub who had been in his care had a good understanding of his duty as a fox.

He thought then of his one and only love Roundears Merriweather. He had been indeed lucky in finding a vixen that was to remain his mate for several years. They had been together a total of five seasons, a quite unusual arrangement for a fox. Freddie remembered with bitterness the day Roundears had been caught in a cruel human trap. The cubs had come running to tell him and he had gone out to be with her in her last moments. He was always grateful that Roundears had been able to die in his paws and thankfully the end hadn't been too painful for her.

He had never taken another vixen as a mate after that and now he went with a small group in which one of his favourite grand daughters was the vixen. The group looked up to him very much because of his hunting skills, his experience and his wisdom, and even though he wasn't the main provider his advice was always sought on important matters.

The events of his schooldays now seemed a dim distant memory and it was only with difficulty that Freddie could recall the names of his various teachers and his many school pals. He had managed to send a number of his cubs to the academy though the curriculum had changed a bit from his day. Not for the better either, he thought, though perhaps he was getting a bit crusty in his old age. He thought fondly of his parents, his fussy hard working efficient mother and his silent stubborn father. He had no doubt that the education they had given him had enabled him to survive to the age that he had, and had enabled him to play a prominent role in his local fox community.

Yes, Freddie had been something of a leader in his day and had been a good organiser of fox events and help for foxes in need. He had been popular with his fellows and well respected and indeed there had been talk of him going forward for greater things and trying for a place as an official fox leader. However that would probably have meant going to live in Dublin, and Freddie was much happier to stay around his beloved Ballynahinch. In any event he had noticed that the influence of the fox leadership wasn't as strong as it used to be and Freddie felt he could do more good by staying with his local foxes. Freddie thought of the many tricks he had been able to play on humans. He had become a somewhat renowned exponent of such tricks. His favourite, which he had perfected almost to a fine art was that of the "goal post ploy" as he called it himself. This was something he had developed in the football field in Clifden which is close to the main road and is bounded on one side by a rather muddy track of ground.

The trick was to wait beside the road until you saw some humans coming in a four wheel drive type of vehicle and then to saunter out onto the road as if you hadn't a care in the world. As sure as duck's eggs is duck's eggs (as his old sainted mother used to say) a human in a four wheel drive who saw a fox sauntering along the road would first of all stop and the take photographs or something and then start chasing the fox with lights flashing and horns blaring. (Humans of the four wheel drive sort, as Freddie called them, were often given to that sort of loud behaviour).

The next part of the ploy was all about timing and it was essential to get it right. Freddie would lead them right through the bit of soft open ground leading to the pitch and just as they were beginning to gain on him he would leap in behind the goal posts and turn around to stare at them with what they would regard as a foolish open-mouthed grin. The boys in the four wheel, who would just now realise where they were, would have to slam on the brakes to avoid hitting the goal posts and in so doing they would dig the large wheels of their vehicle into the soft ground. The curses and swears that would follow this was something that caused Freddie a great deal of amusement, particularly when they would say something like "And will you look at that fool of a fox over there and he not having any idea of the amount of the trouble he's caused us!"

"Yes indeed my clever human beings" Freddie would say to himself, "Perhaps you're not quite as clever as you think" and he would remember his old schoolmaster Reynard from France and how he had always said how important it was to have the laugh at humans whenever possible.

Whenever the foxes in the locality were a bit down in the snout about something, whether it was bad weather or lack of food, Freddie would bring them down to the football pitch, line them up and arrange some kind of a show like this to help them keep their spirits up. Freddie taught all of his cubs this trick and if ever you come across a fox who plays the goal post ploy or some variation of it, you can almost rest assured that he is a descendant of Freddie Fox.

Freddie smiled inwardly to himself as he remembered some of his cubs. Finklesnout with his irrepressible sense of humour, Rosepetal with her gentle and knowing way, Ratcatcher, with his toughness but his soft heart beneath it all. He felt he had had a good life really as he wagged his brush up and down the way foxes do when they are content about something, and he certainly couldn't complain about the way the leaves had fallen for him.

However one of the main regrets of his life was that foxes as a group were simply not as honourable as before, even as they had been when he was a cub. The great fox confraternity of Clonoulty was now like a piece of distant fox history. Freddie remembered well at the time the great excitement that it had caused and the great hopes that it had held for the future. However, many foxes nowadays could hardly even remember what decisions it had reached.

Thomas Jefferson Yowla was now the leader of all the foxes, and had been for several years, and while he was no doubt very popular, Freddie often thought that no-one paid much attention to what he said. Foxes no longer behaved with the sense of honour to themselves or to other animals that Freddie had been taught, and while things hadn't been too bad over the past few years because the winters had generally been good, Freddie wondered what would happen to fox society when a few hard winters came back to back and food became scarce.

A new group of foxes had grown up , called the Steam Tailers, so called because of the way they held their tails at a horizontal angle as opposed to the more orthodox slope, and because they were very fond of taking steam baths, and recommended them as a cure for almost every ailment . Freddie was sad to see that this strange group, despite their foolish doctrines and rites, (I mean who ever heard of a fox taking a steam bath for goodness sake?) had gained a certain popularity, even in Connemara. They didn't seem to believe in any thing much apart from their outlandish steam bath rites and they virtually ignored the code of honour. Freddie thought to himself that it was just typical of when foxes stopped doing what they were supposed to and listening to their fox leaders that all kinds of hare-brained new ideas would start emerging and goodness knew where it would all end up.

He must really stop this he sighed, he was getting much too crusty, and he not even an old aged fox yet. His great great great great grandson, Silken Ears, who was only a cub of six months and of whom he was very fond was always telling him how "badgerish" he was. This was a term a lot of the younger foxes used to describe what Freddie would have called a fox who was stubborn or slow to change his ideas. It was quite a good word really; Freddie had come across more than his fair share of badgers and there was no doubt but that they were a pretty stubborn lot. Well, badgerish or not thought

Freddie, I believe we're in for a bad winter, and I think a lot of our new fangled foxes with their fancy ideas will be responsible for a lot of trouble when it comes.

Last year had been a difficult winter but most foxes had a bit put aside form the previous year's plenty so they didn't suffer too much. Freddie had only seen one or two bad winters but as he sniffed the high mountain air that early October morning he could see that the signs were there for a bad winter coming. Foxes have a way of knowing the pressure of the air, particularly in the high mountain regions, which enables them to predict with a surprising degree of accuracy how wet or how cold the coming months will be. As well as that, they are particularly observant of things like the number of different berries on the trees and bushes, a high number always being the harbinger of cold times to come. Lots of berries would give the birds something to eat, but usually it also meant hard times for the foxes and other large animals. Freddie decided that he'd better go and warn the other members of his small group be expect a difficult time ahead and to make the best preparation that they could.

When he got home (it was still the same burrow that he and Roundears had first set up den in all those years ago, though now quite well furnished and with no end of feathers and other linings) he found that his grand-daughter Roundshanks was giving out crossly to her eldest cub, Willie Hoptail, because he had shown up with his tail held horizontally and evidence (though what evidence Freddie couldn't make out) that he had bathed his tail in steam! He was being warned in no uncertain terms that that kind of behaviour would not be tolerated and that if he didn't mend his ways and pretty darned fast he would be left to fend for himself before the time for dispersal came.

Freddie thought she was being a bit hard on him and

Willie had on a particularly hang fox expression, so Freddie took him aside and tried to explain to him the error of his ways; how the Steam Tailers weren't much good at hunting and would be a pretty useless bunch to be with during a hard winter, how the old fox ways were really much better and would be far more interesting for him to follow and how there really was a lot of very good stuff in the code of honour. Freddie offered to teach him all about the code if he wanted.

Willie listened for a while though with a sullen look on his face and went off saying he would think about it.

"We'll have to watch that one" thought Freddie to himself.

It was pretty difficult to teach young cubs nowadays about the code of honour. Many of them were full of good intentions but there were very few good schools like the academy that he had gone to, and a lot of today's cubs were going around with all kinds of funny ideas in their heads. No wonder they were falling for foolish gangs like the Steam Tailers.

"Anyway , back to business" thought Freddie. At dinner that day Freddie gathered all of the group together and told them of his fears for the coming winter. He formulated a plan that he, Roundshanks and her husband Hawktail would go on "forced hunts " and gather as much food as they could during the remainder of October and the month of November. Any surplus food they would gather they would store under ground and this would give them some surplus during December and January. It was a simple enough plan but you would be surprised how difficult it can be sometimes to get foxes to plan in advance.

However, Freddie had learned over the years how to make everyone feel involved and he was soon able to bring Roundshanks and Hawktail onto his side.

The idea was that by the time the cubs would disperse they would have a store area at the side of the burrow to which they could come back, so that if they got into trouble during the winter they would have something to fall back on. The older cubs were to be left in charge of the burrow while the forced hunts were in progress and with a bit of team work Freddie felt they would make it through.

A hard winter in Ireland can be a difficult and a sad time for both animals and for people. The people of Connemara still talk about "the black 47" and the winter of the big wind, terrible winters that took place in Connemara some years after Humanity Dick had left Ballynahinch castle. In those days many people had starved to death and died of the cold during the long, harsh, wet and terrible winters.
Humans no longer suffer so badly during the winter, but many animals still suffer in the same way when the weather is awful and food is scarce. Fredddie had not been mistaken in his predictions about that winter; Neither he nor any of his friends had ever seen anything quite like it; It rained almost non stop during the entire month of November. Burrows that had been dry throughout living fox memory were flooded out and entire families were thrust out of their homes. Even Freddie's burrow began to show signs of damp and Freddie had to assign two of the cubs to "damming detail" to keep the water out during the worst of the rains.
The advance hunting that Freddie had carried out had stood them in good stead and by the time the rains were abated they were able to catch a few field mice and rats to keep them going. Then during December the time came for the cubs to disperse . Freddie gave them a lot of help in trying to locate a good burrow and showed them some of the building skills he had learned during his young days. He promised to look in on them during the coming months. That was the great thing about not having your own cubs; you could lend a hand during hard

times, and both Roundshanks and Hawktail were very grateful.

The month of December wasn't too bad and Freddie was able to look up a number of his old friends and see how they were getting on . The news wasn't always good and many of the foxes of Freddie's age that year had fallen to "diseases of the damp" as foxes called them. Freddie did what he could, but he was no longer the young fox that he had been and his first priority was to look after his own group. Many of the foxes that Freddie visited that winter began to realise the importance of foxes helping each other when in need and made up their minds that if they survived that winter they would pay a bit more attention to the things Freddie had always been talking about, and that they would try to get involved a bit more in team work and those other things the fox leaders were so keen on.

Freddie and his group survived December but nothing could have prepared them for the cold that was to come during January. The like of it hadn't been seen on Ireland for over fifty years. Entire lakes become frozen over, something Freddie had never seen before, and lake fishing became impossible. Even the tidal inlets became frozen and those foxes who had depended on a bit of food from around the foreshore were in dire straits.

To make matters worse Hawktail, who had never been very strong, developed pneumonia and had to be kept indoors all night. Under no circumstances would Freddie abandon him, even though no fox would have blamed him if he had, and he would go out in the freezing cold every January night to try and find what few mice or rats he could. Always when he came back he would make sure that Roundshanks and Hawktail had something to eat first and he often went without himself to ensure that they didn't starve. He thought wryly of his first night's hunting at the academy and of how they had almost been left without food but for the kindly intervention of good

old Briarpatch.
Despite Freddie's and Roundshank's best efforts however Hawktail was getting weaker and weaker and Freddie knew, and he felt Roundshanks knew also, that it was only a matter of time before he died.

Hawktail was not even to have the dubious pleasure if dying in his own time however. One day, after a night's hunting which had rendered only two mice and a few earthworms (something even hungry foxes find difficult to eat), to be divided between the three of them, Freddie settled down to a day's sleep. At least the burrow which contained so many happy memories for him was still reasonably secure and dry he thought.

Freddie tried not to dream too much about food during the cold and terrible winter, but occasionally thoughts of an easy catch would come into his mind.

Even though hungry Freddie had no difficulty in sleeping, mainly because he was so exhausted. He looked forward to his daily rest during these short winter days and he would decide what he would dream about before going to sleep. This is one of the advantages about being a fox, you get to be able to decide what you are to dream about every night, something that a lot of animals are able to do. Well, after all, it can be pretty hard going being a fox, particularly in the middle of winter, so it's only right that they should be able to get a break from their hard times and be able to seek refuge in dreamland. Freddie didn't want to dream about food because he knew his pangs of hunger would be so much worse when he woke up, so he decided that he would dream about being a carefree fox playing with his cubs and teaching them tricks. After all there was a reasonable chance that a dream like that would come true as soon as this wretched winter was over.

Freddie was about half way through his dream when he heard a scratching sound just above his head. At first he didn't know whether it was part of his dream but soon he could hear the sound of movement just outside the walls of the burrow. Then he saw them! ***SteamTailers! At least a dozen of them coming in through the burrow's escape hatch!***

"Quick" barked Freddie. "Rounshanks! Hawktail! We're under attack! To fang! To fang!"

Freddie quick as a flash was upon the lead Steam Tailer and was going for his throat. Roundshanks and even the sickly Hawktail lost no time either and were into the thick of things with all fangs bared and claws flying quicker than you could say "Foxtail soup" and they started giving the hated Steam Tailers what-for. If there's one thing that can get even the most peaceful of foxes going it's an attack on his burrow! That is regarded in Foxdom as one of the lowest crimes of all and is guaranteed to raise the hackles of any fox or vixen. (If you want my advice, don't ever, ever attack a fox in his burrow!).

Our three gallant heroes, even though severely outnumbered, looked for a while to be getting the better of things and they inflicted many's the hard bite on the enemy, who despite all their force of numbers were clearly not prepared for the fierce resistance they encountered. Freddie had immediately guessed that their only chance was to hem the invaders into one corner of the burrow where their numerical advantage was not quite so useful. This tactic was working quite well and it seemed to be

leading to victory with the lead Tailer looking as if he was about to order a retreat.
Then, just at the critical moment, as often happens in battles, a turning point came. Immediately behind him Freddie heard another noise. It was a second party of Tailers, coming in through escape hatch number two! The three defenders were now surrounded by at least twenty of the enemy.
Freddie couldn't figure out how they had found escape hatch number two because it was extremely well camouflaged on the surface. However there was no time to think about that now. They were surrounded, and the Tailers, even though two of them had been killed, now began to get the upper hand. They began to pick on poor Hawktail because they sensed that he was the weakest of the party. Just like cowardly dogs, thought Freddie.
Soon they had Hawktail on the ground and it was clear that he was done for. He died bravely, and managed to take another one of the Tailers with him before he went, but there was nothing either Freddie or Roundshanks could do to save him. Freddie now realised that their cause was hopeless, and it would be all they could do to get out alive. One warm summer when he had had a bit of spare time on his hands Freddie had built a third escape hatch from the burrow, up a winding part of the root of the oak tree, and he realised that this was now their only hope. They would have to break through a group of four Steam Tailers to make it through, and they might well die in the effort. Still, thought Freddie, what matter if we take a few of those blackguards with us!
With a sudden burst of energy Freddie launched himself ferociously at the Tailer who was standing in front of the secret exit, beckoning to Roundshanks to do the same. The party of Tailers were caught off guard and Freddie was soon able to manoeuvre himself into a position where he could make good their escape. Tossing one of the Tailers aside he pulled the moss covering away from the

concealed entrance.

"Quick" he barked to Roundshanks who herself didn't know of this exit "Up here. I'll cover you!"

The exit had been built by Freddie at the end of a short passageway and was therefore easy for Freddie to defend in that only one Tailer at a time could attack and Freddie was able to cover Roundshanks's retreat without too much difficulty. Then Freddie himself turned suddenly and began to squeeze up the narrow tunnel. All of The Steam Tailers of course made a mad rush to try and grab him and just as he thought he was free one of them managed to grab him by the end of the tail. Freddie was sure that he was caught and if they pulled him back down he knew he needn't expect any mercy. He clung on for dear life, pressing as hard as he could against the dank sides of the tunnel. Then he felt himself slipping back, the tunnel was just too damp! Just as he was about to be pulled down however he managed to grab hold of a piece of tree root and sank his teeth into it, gripping as hard as he could, with the Tailer below hanging off his brush and swinging about eighteen inches above the floor of the burrow. Suddenly the Tailer let go, possibly to get some air, and as soon as he did Freddie bolted off. He had escaped! None of the Tailers of course was fox enough to follow him into the confined space of the tunnel where they knew they would have to face him fox to fox.

As he crawled up the narrow passage Freddie could hear them below, howling madly with victory. Freddie felt grimly that it would be a short lived victory for them, because he knew by the look of them that they probably wouldn't survive that winter and that they wouldn't even know how to keep the burrow itself secure. Little matter now thought Freddie bitterly. He had been thrown out of his own burrow, and by fellow foxes! What a shameful day for Connemara!

The tunnel they were now going through was long and narrow and it took them some time to get to the top.

Roundshanks was in a terrible state when they emerged. She had just witnessed her husband being killed and had been thrown out of her home. Freddie tried to console her as best he could.

"Never mind." he said "At least you have the consolation of knowing that he died fighting and with a look of defiance in his eye. In many ways it would have been worse if he had died from that awful cough he was suffering from. You can always tell any of his cubs that he died honourably."

He tried to be as gentle as he could and he did in fact succeed in cheering Roundshanks up a little. Freddie had always had a good way of cheering up vixens.

Freddie now had to think fairly fast. They were out in broad daylight and would need to find somewhere to hide up for a while. Freddie remembered a small hole in a hedge about a mile distant which might serve as shelter for a few days and he gave Roundshanks instructions on how to get there. He told her he would be along shortly but that he had some unfinished business to attend to first.

When Roundshanks had gone Freddie doubled back and headed for the secret entrance for escape hatch number two. When he got there he was saddened, though not surprised by what he saw. It was just as he suspected. The Steam Tailers had had inside information which enabled them to carry the day. There, standing at the entrance to the escape hatch with a sheepish guilty look on his face and looking about anxiously, was none other than Willie Hoptail!

Freddie crept up behind him without making a sound and then came right out in front of him and bared his fangs. Hoptail nearly jumped out of his skin when he saw Freddie. Even though he was a young fox and Freddie was now getting quite old he had seen some of Freddie's fighting skills and he knew he would be no match for him. In addition he saw a look in Freddie's eye that made him

quiver with fear.
"Why, why Gr.....Great granddad" he stammered as if nothing was the matter. "Look", he then said desperately, "I never knew it was going to turn out like this. They told me there was going to be no violence. How was I to know father was going to be killed?"
Freddie made no reply whatever but just snarled all the more bloodcurdlingly and brought his snout so close to Hoptail's that they were almost touching. Freddie was in a good humour to let Hoptail have it, and if it weren't for the fact that Willie Hoptail bore a slight resemblance to his great grandmother Roundears, it might have turned out the worse for him.
Anyway, Freddie had never attacked another fox before and he wasn't going to start with a relative of his own. Summoning his most withering look and his most disdainful snarl Freddie turned his back on Hoptail and padded off leaving him alone.
Willie Hoptail felt more ashamed than he had ever felt in his life before. He wept bitter fox tears at the thought of what he had done and the look that Freddie had left him with was to haunt him for the rest of his life. Willie Hoptail resolved there and then never to have anything more to do with the wretched dishonourable Steam Tailers and vowed to reform his life from then on. In fact in later life, believe it or not, he was to become something of a champion of the code of honour.
When Freddie got back to the hedge he found Roundshanks waiting anxiously for him, still in a state of agitation. He thought it better not to tell her about Hoptail. She had had enough trouble for one day; to find out that her own cub had betrayed her might break her heart. Freddie knew from experience that vixens often died from broken hearts.
When he got into the shelter Freddie had time to examine some of the wounds he had received. In the excitement of the fight he had paid no regard to his battle scars. He had

received a lot of cuts and had lost a good deal of blood. He had one wound just below the right rear shank that was still bleeding. He licked it as best he could and got the bleeding to stop but it was quite sore. "That will cause me a bit of trouble if I don't get some nourishment soon." he thought.

The priority now was to get themselves fixed up with a permanent place to stay. They had a few temporary burrows around the place but none of these had survived the hard rains of November.

As luck would have it Freddie knew of a three year old fox, not much to look at but honest and a good hunter, who had his own den and who was still looking for a mate. He thought it was time for a bit of old fashioned match making. Desperate times called for desperate measures after all. He told Roundshanks of his plan and she agreed to come and see the fox in question the following night.

The fox's name was O'Halloran, a good honest decent chap who was beginning to think he had left it a bit late in the season to find his year's companion. He was very taken with Roundshanks and as luck would have it Roundshanks took rather a fancy to him as well. That was fortunate thought Freddie, because if a vixen doesn't fancy a potential mate no power in the world will make her hitch up with him; they can be notoriously wilful like that.

O'Halloran (a somewhat unusual name for a fox you might think but there's a story behind that) invited them both in for a drink of wild berry juice to celebrate the occasion. His den was quite humble and nothing compared to what they had just left but O'Halloran was generous and Freddie felt that Roundshanks would be happy with him.

Freddie had not mentioned the events of the previous day to their host as he did not wish to appear to be throwing themselves on his mercy, but when he heard of what had happened to them he very generously insisted that

Freddie would stay in his den for the rest of the winter. Freddie pretended to agree, but he decided to himself, given the rather rushed nature of the mating, that it could well put a strain on the relationship if he were to stay. Also he felt that they would have a much better chance of surviving the remainder of that hard winter if they didn't have him to worry about. For that reason, two days later, after scratching a good-bye note for them on the ground, Freddie crept away in the middle of the day. The winter was hard, cold and bitter, and for the first time in his life, Freddie Fox was totally alone.

CHAPTER 10

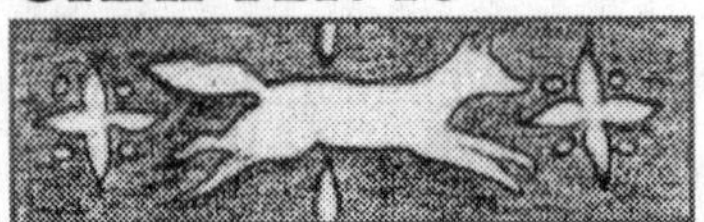

A LIGHT IN THE DISTANCE.

It was early February when Freddie went off on his own to survive as best he could. Usually things in Ireland begin to brighten up a bit by mid February and Freddie was banking on this happening. However the 15th February came and went and there was no improvement in the weather. Freddie had buried one or two things over the years in case of dire emergencies but he had soon exhausted this meagre life's savings and by the third week in February he was staring starvation straight in the face.

His renowned hunting skills stood him in good stead, and he was still able to catch the odd mouse and stoat, but there was no doubt, he was not as fast as he used to be, and with each passing day he was getting weaker and slower. The absence of a safe dry burrow was an additional burden and he used to lay his weary head wherever he could, sometimes taking chances that he wouldn't be discovered by wandering dogs or groups of pine martens. He knew that in his present state he would be no match for a dog and he used to sleep only fitfully for fear that he would hear a pack of dogs coming. Indeed on one occasion he was only saved when an approaching pack of dogs was given away by one pup who started howling when they were about a hundred yards away from where he was sleeping. Freddie was up like a shot and off before they caught scent of him. He was lucky in that he was down wind of them, and he padded away as silently as he could as they went off in a different direction. Two of them were greyhounds, and there was no doubt that if they had caught scent of him that he

would never have been able to outrun them in his weakened state and he would have fallen to the terrible fate that befalls so many foxes in the wild.
The wound below his right rear shank was not healing very well and this slowed him down considerably in hunting. The temporary resting holes he used to stay in were not very stable and with the wet windy weather they were prone to collapse so that he was on the run quite a lot even during the day.

He had one lucky break towards the end of February when there was one fine day and he came across two human beings having a pic-nic on a bench overlooking the bay near Clifden. They were leaving a lot of food on their bench and Freddie was so mad with hunger that he threw caution to the wind and went right up behind them and grabbed three slices of bread and ran off.
To his surprise the humans did not chase after him and indeed when they left, they left behind some other pieces of food including some bits of ham and some sweet tasting things that Freddie had never had before but which he was certainly glad of.
If Freddie didn't know better he would have said that the humans had left the food for him on purpose! But that would have been a pretty silly idea. Freddie checked the bits of food very carefully in case they were drugged. He had heard of this human trick and knew that you couldn't be up to their cleverness. He then took the food as far away as he could before eating it just in case they were hiding close by and were waiting to grab him as soon as his guard was down and he started eating. This little windfall kept him from death's door for a few days but it wasn't long till the severe pangs of hunger were back again.
There was no point in looking for help from other foxes at that time. Not only had the tradition of helping one's neighbour fox almost gone, (despite Freddie's best

efforts), but apart from that there wasn't a fox in all of Connemara who had a bit of spare food at that time. Many foxes, particularly older foxes met a cold, hungry and lonely death during that awful winter, and indeed it was to be spoken of in fox lore for many years to come.

The first of March came and still there was no sign of a change in the weather. March usually brought a bit of relief in that the mad March hares began to emerge, swanning about the place like perfect fools trying to attract mates, and usually they were reasonably good prey for a patient fox who had reasonable hunting skills. In a normal year Freddie could expect to catch a good plump March hare every second day or so. This year however he just wasn't fast enough. His wound had come back and he had lost three hares by the skin of his fangs by just not having enough speed. He only managed to catch one hare in early March and that an old scrawny one that he was clever enough to chase into a shallow stream. By the second week in March Freddie was literally starving. He had lost so much weight he was almost a walking skeleton. Definitely however the weather was beginning to get a bit warmer. Freddie knew that if only he could survive another week or so that he just might make it. The mice would begin to come out of country houses and they were usually easy prey. Some of the larger insects would also begin to come out of the ground, and even though they were horrible to the taste they might prevent starvation. He was beginning to think that he might just survive to see another Spring.
It was then that the worst storm ever to hit Connemara in living or dead fox memory struck with a ferocity that left both animal and human reeling.

Freddie was half way up Ben Lettery as night was falling when he began to notice a sharp drop in pressure. Looking out towards the sea he could see dark, threatening looking clouds moving quickly from the Atlantic ocean, full of menace. He could see the birds flitting about nervously and heading down for the low ground where they might find a bit of shelter. He knew he would have to get down quickly himself. If the storm was as bad as it looked he knew that the small copse of young Ash trees he had been staying in for the last two weeks would be no protection at all and he tried to guess the wind direction to see if he could figure a way of hiding behind a stone wall or some other shelter to avoid the worst of the weather.

The wind when it came fell down on the coast of Connemara like a roaring lion falling on its prey. It howled over the mountains and along the treetops, sending the few remaining birds flying in all directions. It howled along the roofs of houses warning human beings to stay indoors or to come out and be devoured. It brought many's the roof with it and many's the human den was wrecked in that awful storm.

It howled along the coastline sending ships and small boats pounding against the shore and sailors to their merciless doom.

It roared through Connemara's small towns, sending slates crashing down into the broad streets of Clifden. It sent the bravest of humans frightened to their beds where they cowered under their blankets, covering their heads and listening to the awful power raging outside, shaking their walls and rattling their windows.

It sent furious waves dashing against the small cottages at Roundstone and hurling rocks the size of footballs against the boarded up windows.

The few mice that had begun to emerge from the comfort of their winter lodgings in country houses were sent scurrying back under drains and floorboards to peep out in terror at the raging tempest outside.

Huge Oak trees that had stood for hundreds of years

providing food and shelter for generations of animals and birds were uprooted and overturned like giant colossi creaking to their destruction, sending whole families scampering to avoid being crushed.
The rains that came with the storms were such as had never been seen before in Connemara. The levels of streams rose two feet in the space of a few hours. The small neat homes of otters and pine martens were flooded out before they could gather their few belongings and their young were sent sailing down streams that had become torrents, to save themselves as best they could. Roads were flooded and isolated communities of humans were stranded for days on end, not knowing would they ever see peace and harmony again.

While these dreadful tempests roared and crashed, a poor starving and dying fox was crouching beneath a four foot high stone wall in terror of his life. Freddie had correctly guessed the direction of the wind and had headed for a wall giving a bit of shelter in the right direction. His copse of Ash trees had of course been flattened in the first moments of the storm and though the wall gave him some protection from the wind it gave him little or none from the torrential rains and he was soon drenched to the skin and shivering pitiably.
He could feel his cough getting worse and all around him he could hear signs of disaster and damage; trees falling, slates and branches being sent clattering along the ground ready to kill stone dead any creature which came into their paths, rivers and streams bursting their banks and taking the Lord knew what with them.
Freddie crouched as close to the base of the wall as he could. Suddenly he heard a creaking sound overhead and he could see the entire wall moving. It was about to collapse!
Drawing on what little strength he had left, he dashed straight forward just in time to avoid being crushed. The

large stones went scattering in all directions and one of them caught him just below his leg wound, causing him to yelp with the pain.

Freddie limped off, wandering about aimlessly. He had no idea what to do or where to go. The awful noise, the eddying winds and the billowing clouds, blocking out both stars and moon, made him lose all sense of direction and soon he was completely lost. He was finally out of ideas about how to survive any longer or what he could do to give himself a chance of lasting even another few days. His wound was now bleeding badly and he knew that he would not be able to hunt anything until it healed. He also knew that unless he got some food that night that not only would his leg not heal, but that he would die of starvation and cold.

Yes, the game was finally up, Freddie realised sadly. He thought over his heroic struggle to survive that awful winter and felt cheated after having almost come through that he was now falling at the final hurdle. He had just allowed himself a bit of hope that with the weather picking up he might indeed have seen another Spring, but now he knew that he would die that terrible night out in the open, far from his home and his loved ones.

It would have been nice, he thought, to have been able to die peacefully or in the paws of a loved one, but such things were not to be for him. At least he wasn't going to die in a trap or being savaged by dogs. He had managed to avoid that.

He thought again of the main events of his life, his school days, his first family, Clonoulty, his life-long mate Roundears, his many cubs. He thought of the great hopes he had had for Foxdom, and of how he had seen things go so badly wrong. And now it was all going to end here on this wind-swept, rain sodden night.

Freddie wondered what death would be like. As a cub he

had often heard older foxes talk about a light that a fox will see just before he dies, a kind of light that welcomes him into the next world. Most foxes don't really understand these things, but Freddie was now so exhausted that he felt that whatever was in store for him would be better than what he was going through at present.

Freddie then saw a white light ahead of him and he began to limp towards it. It was a bright kindly light in a small clearing with a smooth flat area in front of it and a great Oaken door to one side. That must be death's door he

Freddie Fox goes to meet his destiny.

thought. He had often heard that expression being used before, and now he knew what it meant. As Freddie dragged himself toward the light, for some reason the words of Clarion came back to him from all those years ago at Clonoulty; "Always trust in providence. Always trust in Goodness.".
Freddie had never fully understood what these words meant but now they were a source of great comfort to him as he dragged himself forward between the light and the doorway and laid himself down to die.

Freddie was not at the door of death as he thought but at a place that for some reason had always featured in his life, though he had never been there before. For of all the places in the world, the providence that Freddie trusted in had directed a poor, starving, lost and bewildered fox on that blessed St. Patrick's night to the great front door of Ballynahinch castle. Providence however, can lead those brave enough to trust in it into strange and dangerous places, and the old enmity between human and fox was about to bring Freddie to yet another,even more terrible, brush with death. If Freddie were to survive, Providence would have to send more help, and this time that help would have to come from a very strange source indeed.

Mr. Herbert Bannon was up late that night in Ballynahinch castle. He had decided to stay up to see if anything needed to be done to protect the castle from damage during the storm, and anyway he could hardly sleep with all the tremendous noise. He had never seen a storm quite as bad, and even though he felt the old castle had probably withstood worse in its long history, nevertheless it was as well to stay up and keep an eye on things.
He felt a twinge of pity for anyone or anything caught out

in that dreadful weather and he was glad to be inside within the stout walls of Ballynahinch with the wind whistling furiously outside. He put on his glasses and sat behind the desk of the reception room and tried to do a bit of paper work. There was such an amount of work to do in looking after all of the various affairs of a first class hotel like Ballynahinch, but Mr. Bannon was certainly equal to the task.

It was about two o'clock in the morning and Mr. Bannon felt the storm was beginning to abate. He would stay up another half hour or so and then he would turn in for the night.

Just then he noticed a movement out in the front driveway. Looking carefully through his gold rimmed glasses he saw a scrawny miserable looking fox creeping up towards the front door. There had been a lot of fox activity around the castle over the last year or two, thought Mr. Bannon, and they were beginning to make a bit of a nuisance of themselves.

No doubt he had come when he thought everyone would be asleep so that he could root around in the rubbish or worse still break into the kitchen and steal some food.

"I'll just have to deal with him" thought Mr. Bannon in that efficient way of his, and he crept quietly past the front door, past the portrait of Humanity Dick, which he looked at as he passed, and around to the gun room.

He loaded a short bore rifle and took a short cut out through the bar and up again towards the front door. It would be necessary to make an example of this fox he thought.

As he walked up the long corridor from the bar to the front door he was facing the magnificent portrait of Dick Martin who seemed to be gazing down at him with a somewhat accusing look in his disdainful eye. Not to matter. It would be over in a minute he thought. When he got to the front door he opened it and looked down at the pathetic fox crouching helplessly in front of him. He raised his rifle and took careful aim at Freddie's head.

Freddie now realised that he had not passed into the next world, not as yet anyway, and he began to have a vague idea of where he was. He looked up and saw the hard eyes of Mr. Bannon looking down at him along the barrels of one of those deadly firing engines he had seen humans use before. The hard look was just like that he had seen on the eyes of the hunter the first time he had seen a human close up all those years ago during Reynard's class at the academy. It would all be over soon. Mr. Bannon's finger tightened on the trigger.

Just then a very strange thing happened.

The moment Herbert Bannon was about to fire he felt an eerie shiver running down his spine from his neck right down to the small of his back just like, yes, just like the finger of a ghost!

He leapt with fright and turned immediately with gun pointed to see who or what it was. There was no one there. As he was turning back again he stopped dead. Something, some force he couldn't explain, made him raise his head, slowly, fearfully, almost against his will to look at the huge portrait over the fireplace. He gasped with fright. There was no doubt about it. ***The portrait had changed.***

It was hard to say for certain what it was, the body and the pose were the same, but Dick martin was fixing Herbert Bannon with a cold accusing and terrible look that he had never before seen in the painting. It was a look that told him that he was doing something he would regret for ever more if he continued.

Now you may have guessed from my description so far that Herbert Bannon was a practical man. However, when he thought of the many stories he had heard of Humanity Dick's great love of animals he could not shake the feeling, the certainty in fact, that the ghost of Dick Martin had come back through the centuries to our hard, present day world, and was there in the room, beating at the door of his heart.

Mr. Bannon however forced himself to put such thoughts out of his head and turned around and raised his gun once again. What on earth would his friends say if they knew he had been spooked late at night by a fox and an old painting? Just then he noticed the nick behind Freddie's ear. He had a nick like that behind his own ear.

Freddie fox looked up at his would-be killer, wondering what was taking him so long. Then he looked into Herbert Bannon's eyes and he saw something there that he had never seen in human eyes before.

Herbert Bannon put his gun down.

He simply couldn't do it. And the funny thing was he felt a huge sense of happiness and relief that he couldn't do it.

Freddie knew that something had happened, and while he wasn't sure what, he felt that he had received help from a kind and mysterious protector.

He had indeed received help, and from a source that neither he nor Mr. Bannon would ever fully understand.

Mr. Bannon went back to the kitchen after looking around to see that no-one was watching and got Freddie as big a feed of rich food as would have done a family of foxes. He placed it down about two feet in front of Freddie and withdrew behind the front door. I needn't tell you Freddie was taken aback by this turn of events but in the state he was in he didn't need to be asked twice. He wolfed down the food ravenously and then much to his further surprise another plate of that strange sweet food appeared in front of him.

Freddie felt he had found a friend indeed. He knew that in this his hour of terrible need the hand of human kindness had been extended to him. He decided however that he had better not ride his luck, and after he was

finished he headed back into the forest. The worst of the storm had by now abated.
Mr Bannon picked up the dishes he had left out for Freddie and he hoped, and somehow he knew, that he would see that fox again. As he passed back towards the kitchen he took another look at the portrait. The firm wry smile had returned to Dick Martin's face.

Freddie had received help from a strange and unexpected source, but a source as old as time itself. The great humanity and kindness of Dick Martin had made its journey through the long centuries to the front door of Ballynahinch to save a helpless dying and pitiful creature on that awful night of storm. But perhaps its journey also had a greater purpose. Remember old Humanity if some day you come across a cold, wounded, miserable and starving fox, for human kindness saves both the giver and the receiver.

The following morning was the most beautiful that Freddie could ever remember. He had of course seen the calm after the storm before, and perhaps it was the fact that the previous night's storm had been so bad that gave this calm its special quality. There was no doubt that the long terrible winter was now finally over. Birds in Ireland traditionally start building their nests on St. Patrick's day, but they hadn't had much opportunity to start that St. Patrick's day with the awful winds and rains.
However they were certainly making up for it that morning. They were out surveying the damage from the storm and getting on with their business of finding new trees and using the twigs that had fallen to start the construction of new houses. No moping about crying over spilt milk for them thought Freddie. All the other creatures of the woodlands, badgers, pine martens,

stoats, hedgehogs, rats, they were all making plans for getting on with things. You don't have much choice really when you live in the wild but to get on with it.

Freddie found himself a very good sized burrow at the base of an uprooted Ash tree. He was able to make a very convenient escape tunnel along the root of the tree and after only a morning's work he had a passable and dry shelter. This will do to be getting on with he thought, though he had every intention of claiming back his old burrow later on in the Summer when he had regained a little more of his strength.

Freddie had had enough to eat from the night before to last him a while, so he decided to sit down and do some serious thinking.

He sat down in his new burrow and put his wise head to one side the way you often see foxes doing when they have some particularly knotty problem to sort out. Freddie was, quite frankly, puzzled. What had happened to him the night before he felt was undoubtedly the most important event that had happened to him in his life and he felt that it was a part of what some foxes referred to as their destiny.

He had never expected a human to behave to him, or indeed to any fox, in the kindly way that Mr. Bannon had done, (Freddie knew Mr. Bannon both by name and reputation as he had often watched him from the edge of Ballynahinch castle grounds). Freddie had never been inside the grounds of Ballynahinch before, let alone right up to the front door of the castle, but he somehow felt that it was no accident that he had ended up there last night when he was in the tightest corner he had ever been in. Fate was a thing he had heard about when he had been at Clonoulty, and he had little doubt that Fate had played a major part in bringing him to safety the previous night. "Now, what of the future?" Freddie asked himself. The humans had shown themselves to be kindly and good on one occasion, but would they always be so? They were notoriously devious and could weave the most cunningly elaborate plots to ensnare a fox in order to capture him or worse.

Then Freddie thought of the kindly look he had seen in Mr. Bannon's eye the previous night. Freddie had always prided himself in being a good judge of the contents of a creature's eye. You had to be able to tell what the eye revealed if you were to survive in the wild, and Freddie felt that Mr. Bannon's motives were good at heart. And then of course there was the whole thing of the fact that the extraordinary events of last night had taken place at Ballynahinch castle, former home of Humbledrum Dick. Surely there was some significance in that.

Freddie had enough of thinking.(Foxes, though they like to think things out a bit are usually anxious to make up their minds fairly quickly and they often like acting on instinct- It's one of their more endearing traits). He decided as of a sudden that he would have faith in these humans, the same faith that they had shown in him, and that he would go back to the castle again.

He felt in some strange way that he had a duty to go back, as if some purpose was going to be served if he went back. However he made up his mind there and then that he was never going to become one of those "pet foxes" that were supposed to exist in the city. If the humans were going to be good to him all well and good, but he was certainly not going to become one of their trophies the way he had seen poor Sylvester become, and they would have to respect his independence as a fox. So there!

Freddie decided he would leave the dust settle for a while and he went back to Ballynahinch the following day just as night was beginning to fall. He approached from the low hill in front of the castle front door and hid in the branches for a while to observe the scene and to make sure everything was safe before making his presence known. He decided he would wait until he saw Mr.

Bannon before making any moves. When he saw Mr. Bannon through the window he crept up and walked up and down a few times to see if anything would happen. He was about to go away thinking that this business of his destiny being wrapped up with that of the castle was so much duck feathers when sure enough two humans emerged very gingerly, without any guns and carrying bowls of food.

One of them was Mr. Bannon and the other was a young vixen human with a very pleasant look on her face. They placed the food about two feet in front of them and stood there waiting for Freddie to come and take it. Well Freddie wasn't too happy with this I needn't tell you; I mean dash it all, a fox's golden rule is never to get too close to humans and two feet is only about the length of a human arm. Freddie paced up and down nervously without going near the food.

The humans seemed to understand what was going on and they shortly withdrew behind the door and looked out the glass panel. This was a bit better and Freddie now came to take their offerings while keeping a very careful eye out in case there were any sudden moves. When he was finished he raced off into the wild again. There was no point in being too familiar.

Freddie decided he would come back at the same time every day. When he came back the following day the humans seemed to be waiting for him and they had his food all ready. In addition they had a young man who watched Freddie very carefully out through the front window and seemed to be pointing things out to the others. Freddie noticed suspiciously that he was taking a particular interest in his wound (which incidentally wasn't healing at all well and was still very painful) just above the rear right leg.

When Freddie came back the following day the young man was there again watching carefully as before. Freddie approached his food a bit suspiciously this day.

As he was eating he saw something which confirmed his worst fears; There, hidden in the food (and not very expertly hidden I might add) were little coloured things a bit like pigeon's eggs only much smaller.
So, the humans were up to their old tricks eh? Trying to poison him or more likely to drug him so that they could bring him away to carry out their evil experiments on him. Freddie was in a bit of a pickle; if he tried to make a run for it they would almost certainly shoot him, (they probably had their guns trained on him from all angles even now he thought), and if he were to eat these little coloured eggs who knew what might happen? Pretending to eat the eggs he actually hid them in a cavity in one of his large back teeth, and when he was finished the rest of the food he sauntered casually away as if nothing whatever unusual had happened.
When he got back to his burrow however he pulled out the eggs from the cavity and had a good hard look at them and smelled them from all directions. They certainly didn't smell like poison, and Freddie had had so much experience of detecting human poison in his lifetime that he was considered something of an expert in the field.
But what could they be for if not poison? They certainly weren't food. Freddie decided on a middle course. He would eat two of the four eggs he had found and if they did him no immediate harm he would go back to the castle again the next day.
Freddie tried this and it seemed to work allright . The eggs, which were in his food every day, didn't seem to do him any harm. One thing he did notice though is that his wound began to heal up very quickly, much more quickly than any deep wound of his had ever healed before.

In time Freddie began to trust the humans of Ballyanahinch castle a bit more, and he began to allow them to come quite close to him. He began to get to know human ways and human personalities quite well and he had a very good knack of knowing which humans he could trust and which ones had to be watched. Mr. Bannon he had special regard for and it was Mr Bannon who gave him his human name of Freddie, by an astonishing coincidence the same as his name in fox language!

As I've already mentioned it had sometimes happened in the city that a fox had gotten close to human beings, and had been fed by them. However such a thing was totally unheard of in the west of Ireland, indeed in any rural part of the world it is exceedingly rare for a fox to have regular contact with humans.

For this reason Freddie's fame spread far and wide and he was soon the talk of all of Connemara. A lot of the farmers in the area couldn't believe that a fox would get close to humans and not attack them (When did you ever see a fox attack a human being?) and people began to come to Ballynahinch just to see this extremely rare event; the wonder fox of the west!, The bold fox of Ballynahinch! The magnificent Freddie!

Children in particular began to show a great interest in Freddie, and many of the local children and children from Galway used to come out to visit him.

Foxes being the quiet sorts of animals they are, Freddie found this new found fame a bit of a strain, but he made the sacrifice as he realised that the destiny he had wondered about that morning after the storm appeared to be to bring the world of the fox and the world of the human closer together; to encourage a kind of *détente* between the human and the vulpine worlds.

One of the peaks of Freddie's fame came when the television cameras arrived one day and filmed him together with a group of local children. A line of children was asked to arrange themselves in a semi-circle around the front door of Ballynahinch and Freddie came up to each one in turn and took a bit of food from right out of their hands! The likes of this had never been seen in Ireland before and soon children all over the country began to take a special interest in foxes and began to realise what wonderful animals they are.

It would be wrong to think that Freddie spent all of his time after the storm in the company of humans however. He spent no more than perhaps a half an hour a day with his human friends. The remainder was spent in the wild and in the company of other foxes. After the extraordinary events that had happened to Freddie he became something of a celebrity among his fellow foxes. There was no doubt that many foxes had suffered severely during the great storm and some of them began to see that if they had been a bit more concerned in looking out for one another and in behaving a bit more honourably towards one another they might have had a few more resources when the great storm came.

Freddie was held up as an example of a fox who had stuck to his principles and in particular to the code of honour, and who by trusting in providence had come good in the end despite the many difficulties he had faced. All of the foxes understood the great good that Freddie was doing by promoting better relations between humans and foxes and they thought he was frightfully brave by going into what they saw as "the valley of death". They certainly didn't begrudge Freddie the food that he got; he deserved it after the difficulties he had had, and they admired the way that Freddie never became a pet fox, always keeping the humans at a certain distance and never letting them become too familiar.

Many of the Connemara foxes began to have another look at the code of honour and at things like team hunting and helping other foxes in need when times were hard. Freddie, even though he had no ambitions to become a fox leader, was regarded as the unspoken leader of Connemara. Indeed, like Humanity Dick before him, he became known among his fellows as "The King of Connemara" and no great decision would be made, about territories, tail styles , fishing rights or other weighty matters without first consulting "Oracle Freddie" as he was also known.

On the subject of tails you might ask what ever became of the Steam Tailers.

Some time after he had started going to the castle Freddie decided that the time had come to reclaim his original burrow. He gathered together a few stalwarts (including, believe it or not Willie Hoptail), and went to pay the Tailers a visit. When they arrived they found a party of only six pathetic looking Steam Tailers present. They had fought like mad with each other throughout the winter and had let the burrow get into a right state of disrepair. When Freddie and his party showed up the remaining Tailers had taken one look and scurried off in terror without even putting up so much as a decent fight. Steam Tailing died a pretty rapid death in Connemara shortly after this for another reason. It transpired that the regular Steam baths together with the herbal mixtures they used, had the rather unpleasant side effect of making all of the fine brush fur in a fox's tail fall out! The Steam Tailers shortly became known as the "No Tailers" and became the laughing stock of all of Connemara. Soon no self respecting young fox would have anything to do with them and the whole movement disappeared without trace.

"And good riddance" thought Freddie fox.

Freddie the Fox pictured during his early days at Ballynahinch.

Freddie with the author and Mr. Des Lally at Ballynahinch

A wary Freddie approaches a well intentioned lady.

CHAPTER 11

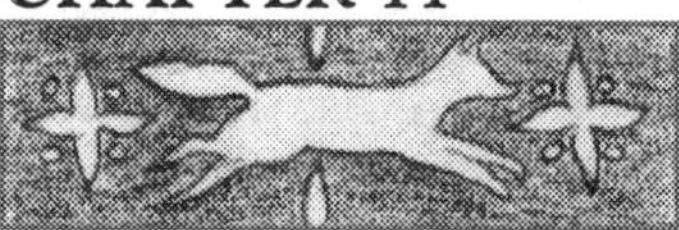

THE STRANGE DREAM OF FREDDIE FOX

The fame of Freddie fox spread far and wide throughout the length and breadth first of Connemara, and then of Ireland. People who would hear of his story would smile inwardly to themselves, and as they watched this beautiful and clever animal on their television screens or read about him in their newspapers they would think that foxes were a pretty decent sort of animal and would think that maybe they weren't such pests or such enemies as they had always believed.

The last time I was in Connemara and stayed at Ballynahinch Freddie was still going strong, still charming all the visitors and causing them to marvel at his beauty and cleverness. He never did silly things like tricks or making silly faces, and he never allowed strangers to become too familiar with him. In a way this was part of his charm. He wasn't like one of those tame circus animals, pleasant though they are, and he always maintained his wildness and his mystery in human eyes. The thing about Freddie that everybody liked was that he was still very much his own fox, a wild fox who had decided for reasons of his own that he was going to allow people to get close to him and that he was going to get to know people a little better.

A lot of the information Freddie gleaned from his contact with humans he brought back to his fellow foxes in the wild. Things like how quickly a human would react to sudden movements, how to tell a kindly human from a wicked one, what young humans were like etc. etc.

The whole idea of any humans being kind was something of which many of Freddie's colleagues were pretty

sceptical, I can tell you, and if it were anyone other than Freddie, whom they all knew to be a fox of integrity, that was telling them these stories about humans, they would probably have given him fairly short shrift indeed.
Freddie however had long mastered the great fox art of being able to hold an audience spellbound, and during the winter and especially during the fox's fallow period of September, Freddie was a sought out story teller and his tales of his contact with humans became something of a Connemara attraction, with foxes travelling long distances so that they could enjoy a session of Freddie's interesting and diverting tales of human beings.
Freddie had never lost his ability to cheer up his fellow fox and foxes who came to Freddie with the cares of the world on their shoulders usually left feeling much more happy and optimistic, as if a weight had been taken from them. Freddie always had a way of attaching a moral to his stories that would show the other foxes that even though they were hard pressed at times that things would usually turn out for the best, especially if they trusted in providence.

One day, as winter was approaching Freddie suddenly began to feel certain changes coming over him, not so much physical changes as changes in the way he thought about things and the way he felt about things. Freddie had heard about these feelings before. He wasn't sure if he was dying but if he was he had no regrets. He had had a long and happy life. Certainly he had had his difficulties and his troubles, his pains and his sorrows, but then it wouldn't have been much of a life if he hadn't. Freddie decided that it was time for him to go to a quiet place of his own. He decided to leave his burrow, which he left to one of his many great great great grand children. He had set aside another burrow where he knew he wouldn't be disturbed in a quiet location at the edge of an old disused stone well. He had always had a knack of

finding convenient places for building safe burrows and he had built this one secretly about a year before.
He sat down in his burrow and began to think of the many events of his past life.
He thought of the many friends he had had . One by one he remembered them; his school pals, Roundears, his many cubs and their cubs and later on the many human friends he had made, which ones he could trust and which he would be wary of. He thought about his two lives, his first up until the night of the storm and his second after he had come to Ballynahinch. In a funny way, what his father had spoken to him about that night long ago when they had been out walking was particularly true of him; that a thing had to die before it could live. Freddie felt that his first life had indeed died so that his second could live.
In no time at all Freddie was fast asleep, dreaming about the many pleasant events of his two lives.
Shortly after falling asleep he was woken by the feel of a human hand around the back of his neck. In all his time he had never let a human being touch him around the back of the neck and he jerked his head up ready to snarl or to bite.
However when he saw who it was he knew instinctively that he was in no danger. The man who stood in front of him had a kind look on his face. Freddie knew that he had seen him somewhere before but he couldn't think exactly where. The man was big and powerfully built with a determined and firm look on his face. He was dressed in strange but very elegant clothes and Freddie couldn't figure out how he had gotten into his burrow.
The man beckoned to Freddie to follow him and Freddie did so. Suddenly he was in the midst of a great hall, just like the great hall in Ballynahinch would have been years ago. Freddie then remembered where he had seen the kindly man before.
One winter's evening when he had been a little early in

coming to Ballyanhinch, Mr. Bannon had gone off to get him something to eat and had left the great door slightly ajar. Summoning up his courage Freddie had carefully poked his head in the front door. His eye was immediately drawn to a striking portrait over the fireplace of a hard but kind looking man in middle age and dressed in the clothes of a bygone era. It was the same man that was now leading him forward into this great and splendid hall. When he got into this great hall Freddie found many of the friends he had just been dreaming about. There was his old teacher Slimlegs Whitepatch, looking as formidable as ever, there was his father Henry, there was his old friend Redeye. They all came up to him with a word of welcome. Then the group parted and there was Roundears with her slightly silly smile and her beautiful rounded ears.

Just as Freddie was meeting his old friends a fox called Ratcatcher who was sleeping in his burrow in Gort jumped up as if something had just brushed along the back of his neck. He was overcome with a feeling of sadness, and though he couldn't explain it he knew that somehow, somewhere he had lost a friend and protector.

That night if you were walking along the edge of the Owenmore river you would have heard a low sad wailing sound. You might have thought it was the wind, but if you were a fox you would have recognised the sound of the Fox *Banshee.* It wailed gently along the river bank and up to Derryclare lake. It wailed along the slopes of Ben Lettery and fox cubs who were in their dens covered their heads and crept up to their mothers for comfort.
Many of the older foxes knew what the sound was and felt saddened in one sense though happy in another. Even some humans who heard it were filled with an unaccountable sense of sadness and knew that they had lost a friend.

The sound continued wailing up and down the hills of Connemara, the twelve Bens, where Freddie had spent so much of his lifetime playing and hunting. It rolled sadly up the moors and then getting stronger it went out to the wild blue Atlantic ocean and died out over the crashing waves.
On certain winter nights you can hear it still if you walk, alone, up the hills of Connemara.

Mr. Bannon heard the sad wailing sound and was also filled with sadness. He looked out the front window of Ballynahinch castle and wondered why Freddie, usually so punctual, had not turned up that night. He happened to glance at the great portrait over the fireplace.
Humanity Dick Martin looked down on the entrance hall of Ballynahinch as he had done for so many long years. That night Mr. Bannon could have sworn that he wore a gentler if a sadder smile.

THE END

CAN YOU SOLVE THE MYSTERY OF FREDDIE FOX ?

As you may have guessed, the tale of Freddie the Ballynahinch Fox, while based on true events, is also an allegory with a hidden message. To help you find this allegory, the story contains a number of anagrams.An anagram is a word, or groups of words which if it has its letters re-arranged will spell a diferent word or group of words. For example "cart-horse" is an anagram of "orchestra". The names of characters or places in the book, might, if you change their letters or initials around, give you completely different names and help you to solve the mystery. I have to admit, the anagrams are pretty tricky, but if you think of the story of the book and its tale, then the hidden meanings may well occur to you. There are a total of ten anagrams, and the first correct entry I receive will win a self catering weekend in Connemara. Who knows who you might meet there?

To help you out a bit I have numbered the anagrams and shown the number of letters in each one. The anagrams are numbered in the order they appear in the book.(See overleaf) . You must enter on the attached form and send your answers to me at Clifden, Corrofin, Co. Clare. I'm afraid I won't be able to reply to each entry but if you send a stamped addressed envelope I will let you know how many anagrams you got right (though I won't tell you which ones!). Remember, they are pretty tricky but a hint is that your grandparents may be able to help you with some of them. Also **remember the story**.
Last date for receipt of entries 31st of July 1998.

Each _ here represents a letter in each anagram. Fill in the letters over the dashes to solve the mystery. The dashes on the left show the words as they appear in the story.

✂ Cut along this line

1. _______ is an anagram of _______, though this is a pretty tricky one to start.
2. _______ ___ is an anagram of __________
3. ____ ____________ is an anagram of ________ ________, though this doesn't have much to do with the story.
4. _______ is an anagram of _______
5. _________ is an anagram of _________
6. ________ is an anagram of ________
7. ________ is an anagram of ________
8. ___ ______ is an anagram of _____ ____
9. ________________ is an anagram of _______ _________
10. ______ _______ is an anagram of _____________

Name:...
Address:..
....
....

You might also wish to enclose a sentence explaining the "hidden" meaning of the story. But even if you don't do this if you are the first to get all the anagrams right you will still win the prize. Make sure you include your name and address in the area provided and remember you must enter on the form provided by cutting it out of the book. Good luck. Michael Leahy.